SPIGWORTH POND

John Saunders

Published by New Generation Publishing in 2016

Copyright © John Saunders 2016

Cover design by Toni Hausler

ISBN 978-1-78507-723-4

The author asserts the moral right under the Copyright, Designs and Patents Act 1988 to be identified as the author of this work.

All Rights reserved. No part of this publication may be reproduced, stored in a retrieval system or transmitted, in any form or by any means without the prior consent of the author, nor be otherwise circulated in any form of binding or cover other than that which it is published and without a similar condition being imposed on the subsequent purchaser.

www.newgeneration-publishing.com

New Generation Publishing

DEDICATION

Spigworth Pond is dedicated to my dear wife Carole, and the angling writers and journalists who have tickled my fancy over the years:

>Andy Little
>Chris Yates
>Colin Dyson
>Frank Barlow
>George Sharman
>Jim Gibbinson
>John Bailey
>Kevin Maddocks
>Neville Fickling
>Rod Hutchinson
>Tim Paisley

Many thanks to Toni Hausler for the artwork and cover design, and to my friend Joey Tait for introducing me to Toni.

© John Saunders 2015

SPIGWORTH - AN INTRODUCTION

If you are looking for an angling book with original top tips on how to catch your favourite species of coarse fish, you have just picked up the wrong book. Put it down and find a book, which teaches you how you can 'Be the envy of all anglers in your club by catching humungous sticklebacks on my super rigs and power baits!'

However, if you like the idea of a book, which has humorous stories about a coarse fishing club with oddball members, this one, could be right up your street!

As with my first novel The Vernham Chronicles, I knew that Spigworth would be difficult to write. I don't mean difficult in a complicated way, this book is easy to read, but I knew from the start that its appeal may only be to a rather unique reader. The aim was to not only write a novel for the angler who likes a bit of a titter on the bank while waiting for the buzzers to go off, but also a non angling reader with a silly sense of humour, not familiar with angling and its jargon. For this reason, I have deliberately tried to avoid overcomplicating things by being too technical. This book is not for taking seriously; so please don't be too analytical? In the same way as science fiction ignores scientific fact, angling fiction deserves the right to bend angling fact.

All anglers who belong to fishing clubs will be familiar of certain members and their eccentric ways; The Spinfield Coarse Angling Club (S.C.A.C.) is no different.

The story starts at the opening of the 1975 – 1976 coarse fishing season. The S.C.A.C. began renting Spigworth

Pond in the early 1950s; by the 1970s, the club was truly established.

Spigworth is a collection of short humorous stories about S.C.A.C club members and their antics throughout the nine months of a coarse fishing season, and not always about fishing. The characters are quirky, quaint and charming and not the usual type of person one would meet by the side of a pond or riverbank.

I hope you have as much fun meeting the characters as I have had writing about them.

Pour a large single malt, or whatever your tipple may be, and relax into a book guaranteed to melt away the woes of the day!

Cheers!

John.

CHAPTER 1

A NEW SEASON AT SPIGWORTH POND

It was 7:30pm June 15th 1975 at Spigworth Pond, and 23 very keen coarse anglers were excited after 3 months enforced angling abstinence to wet their lines at the stroke of midnight; June 16th is the dawn of the new coarse fishing season.

The close season for coarse fishing starts on March 15th and ends June 15th and is supposed to benefit the fish; giving them 3 months peace from the bombardment of lead weights, floats and baits, while they get down to the serious business of making whoopee! The close season for many coarse anglers has seemed to be a bit of an anomaly, as some of the fish such as carp and tench seem to choose June or July to 'get down and get dirty'. However, being fish that originate from warmer climes, they choose when the water temperature is right for them, and are not governed by any man made legislation. For any angler who has set up their swim, or favoured fishing pitch for the night or very early morning, it can be very frustrating sitting there trying to catch a fish when they've got huge barrel sized carp thrashing away in the water in front of them. Sometimes, one may encounter getting a soaking with pond water and carp spawn as the piscatorial lunkers procreate! In addition, many coarse anglers have long believed that the close season was purely devised as a method of keeping coarse anglers off the banks, so that the financially better off game fishermen could whip the water to froth with their fly lines in pursuit of salmon or trout. The name 'coarse' was awarded as a derogatory term for fish that were not so delicately flavoured, or having a slightly earthy taste; and so any angler that fished for these fish became known as a coarse fisherman. Game fishermen could pay hundreds of pounds per season to fish the salmon or trout beat, and so less wealthy coarse fishermen were not welcome. Before going on too much about the then farcical close season rules, it did seem rather unfair that coarse anglers were forced to hang up their rod bags, particularly as most of the ponds they fished didn't hold any trout in them in the first place. In the second place, if you did stock these ponds with trout, they would probably be gobbled up by very hungry pike anyway! It would be many years before this close season madness would eventually be readdressed, and money greedy fishery owners would open their coarse ponds during March 15th until June 15th for any method trout fishing, where any angler could fish with any form of tackle or bait and enjoy the fishing all year round. After all this silliness in the latter half of the 1990s, the Environment Agency conceded that, the close season should only apply to rivers, canals and streams. Still waters that were landlocked and held no game fish were okay for fishing forever! Some coarse angling clubs still hold with the close season today on their still waters. The coarse angler actually respects and cares for the fish, and finds pleasure in gently returning the catch alive to fight another day, not bang them on the head with a priest and slap them in the oven! So who is the true sportsman?

Back to Spigworth Pond then, 6 feet 5 inches tall and wide, once ginger, now white haired Head Bailiff of the

S.C.A.C. (Spinfield Coarse Angling Club) Mark Gosling, was leaning on the entrance gate to Spigworth Pond with a menacing 'You can't come in until I unlock the gate!' look on his ruddy complexioned face. Mark Gosling never seemed to smile even when catching his personal best fish. Mark was very strange; his head was brimming full of the funniest jokes one had ever heard and he'd still have a stern expression after delivering the punch line to the gag he'd just told you. He thoroughly enjoyed watching The Morecambe and Wise Show on television, even though he sat throughout the show without cracking a smile. One angler once thought he'd seen Mark smile, but it was only acute flatulence that was making the corners of his mouth turn up; once this had passed, Mark would be pokerfaced again. Just about every angler of the S.C.A.C feared Mark coming around to check their fishing permits and rod licences, because he always looked as though he was going to beat you up whether you'd remembered your licence or not. Mark was always being followed by 'Squirt' whose real name was Peter Burt. Peter Burt, 4 feet 11 inches tall, would always seem to be at Mark Gosling's side, whether it was at an AGM, fishery close season work party, fishing, or sometimes in the supermarket. No one was ever certain if Mark approved of this situation or not, he never told Peter to leave him alone or stick around. Peter was just always there! Maybe Mark enjoyed the hero worship deep down inside his miserable bulk. Hero worship? Maybe, but truth to tell, Peter was scared stiff of Mark Gosling and it made sense to be on his side, even if he wasn't aware that Peter was there most of the time.

Amongst the happy throng of childishly excited anglers was William Parsons, a big fan of Fred J Taylor and his great piscatorial writings. Such a huge fan of Fred J Taylor was William that he even copied his hairstyle. Anyone who knows of Fred J will know that he was bald on top even as a young man. William shaved the top of his head in tribute to Fred J, but couldn't quite go the whole hog and have all his long blonde hair cut off after spending years trying to convince his mum and dad that not only girls wear their hair long. Then one day in his local pub not long after receiving a pair of black eyes from a fight in a nightclub, a youngster wielding an autograph book approached him. The youngster told him that Do the Strand was his favourite song and Roxy Music were his favourite band and 'Can I have your autograph please Brian?' After having his identity mistaken for Brian Eno, William braved the barbershop and went for a short back and sides. The anglers of Spigworth Pond were quite used to seeing other anglers turn up with a spiky orange 'Bowie cut' or a Marc Bolan 'Corkscrew' perm; but William Parsons was possibly and unintentionally, the freakiest hairstyle owner to have caught tench in the lily pads on Fred J's 'lift method'! William's nickname was 'Badger Bill' incidentally.

Then there was Chris Moffat the gudgeon specialist. The gudgeon, a sweet little cheeky faced fish was more common in rivers and streams and rarely caught much bigger than a couple of ounces. However, the S.C.A.C. decided to stock this little fish in Spigworth Pond and they thrived, growing to a fair size. Chris Moffat had a knack in catching specimen fish. To his credit he had landed roach to 2 lbs, perch to 3 lbs 5oz, bream to 7 lbs, carp to 21 lbs 15oz, tench to 5 lbs and pike to 20 lbs from various venues. But the fish that captured his affection was the gudgeon, and one day in the 1969 season he caught the gudgeon of his dreams; *3oz & 5 drams exactly (according to the recently calibrated scales of the local fishing tackle shop Ken Truman's) and this inspired Chris to write a book on big gudgeon fishing tips called Gudgeon Frenzy. The book sold poorly.

The agreed time to let anglers on to Spigworth Pond to choose their swims on the eve of the coarse fishing season was 8:00pm; the anglers' watches crawled begrudgingly towards that time. Mike Gosling looked at his watch and observed that it was 7:57pm. He then rolled a cigarette and glowered at the expectant piscators just to make them feel uneasy.

"It must be nearly 8 o' clock now Mark?" said Chris Moffat.

"It's only 8 'o clock when Mark says it is!" retorted little Peter Burt, puffing his insignificant chest out as though he was Mark Gosling's guardian.

"Nearly time!" said Mark Gosling pulling off a stray bit of hand rolling tobacco that had become semi adhered to his bottom lip. Mark Gosling flicked the tobacco strand away with his thumb and forefinger. The tobacco strand carried by a slight breeze flew straight into the corner of Peter Burt's eye. Not trying to make too much fuss and upset his hero Mark, Peter removed the offending tobacco strand from his smarting eye with the tip of a finger and pretended to be winking.

"Alright then Mark?" said Peter, his eye streaming with tears.

By Mark Gosling's watch, it was 8:00pm imprecisely and at variance to British Summer Time and everyone else's timepieces.

"8 o' clock!" said Mark, fumbling around in the right breast pocket of his combat jacket, in search for the key to the gate's padlock. For a brief moment, Mark's usual 'bulldog chewing a scorpion' expression almost broke into a look of worry. Mark searched in the other breast pocket of his combat jacket and found nothing. Then he explored all the other pockets of his jacket unsuccessfully. Trying to hide the fact that you are worried when you are worried is difficult at the best of times; but trying not to change the 'miserable bastard' face that Mark wore permanently was even more difficult.

Badger Bill observed the padlock attached to a chain that tethered the gate to the gatepost, the key that Mark was frantically looking for was already in the padlock.

"Ahem! Mark, I think you'll find the key is in the padlock!" Badger Bill pointed out with a certain amount of trepidation.

"What?" said Mark staring at the padlock in disbelief. Mark suddenly burst into uncharacteristic hysterical laughter, accompanied by a rolling about in the stinging nettles.

It would appear that Mark had absent-mindedly left the key in the lock after a mid close season work party and it had been there for quite a while. Squirt made himself feel important by unlocking the gate's padlock and letting the patient anglers onto the banks of Spigworth Pond. One by one, the anglers stepped over Mark's chortling mass, some of them running to get to the swim they wanted to spend the night in. No one but an angler would know how that feeling of release feels when a new coarse fishing season is about to dawn.

The first swim to fight over for carp anglers was Number 1, which was right next to some overhanging Elder tree branches that almost touched the surface of the pond. In

August through to September, the little elderberries would occasionally fall into the pond to be enjoyed by fish. Roach particularly liked these little black drops of manna falling from heaven. Oddly enough, none of the anglers on Spigworth Pond ever thought about using the berries as hook bait.

Every angler had their favourite swim to fight for, but one swim that none of them could fish in was Greenie's Number 9. Bob Green was a colourful character who used to favour swim Number 9 as he felt that a deep trench on the edge of the lily pads 10 yards out at the bottom of this swim was the place to put a bait to catch a very big carp. Bob was a very good angler in general, but his knack of catching carp was the abject envy of other anglers on Spigworth Pond. When it was considered that the best most anglers could do was to land ten carp in a season from this very difficult water; Bob managed twenty-six carp! Four of his carp weighed over 20 lbs, the best weighing 23lbs 7oz! This talk of 20 pounders would most probably not impress many carp anglers of the 21st Century; but in most ponds and lakes in the 1970s, these fish were giants. Richard Walker's 44lb Clarissa and the name Redmire would have seemed more like folklore than reality. Despite all of Bob's success, one carp eluded him. Affectionately named Fatso, and thought to be over 30lbs, she hadn't been caught since 1966 when she only weighed 5lbs or so. Of course, she wasn't called Fatso then, but when Bob caught her whilst fishing for tench in June 1964 he observed an unusual large black spot she wore on top of her head. 8 years on from that day, Bob saw her again during the close season in May when he was leaning over the pond watching carp from a branch of a tree that he had climbed. With Spigworth Pond's typically clear water, Bob could see every detail of the lake bottom and its inhabitants. Slowly, out from a gap in the bank side reed mace, Fatso appeared with the grace of a whale, making her way for the cover of the lily pads in swim Number 9. For the next 2 years, Bob became obsessed with Fatso and devoted all his time in pursuit of her. He tried various large baits to prevent the smaller carp from being able to pick them up and waste his time catching fish he would rather not catch. Large parboiled potatoes were used to good effect but Bob wanted to be able to put a hook bait out there that would last a long time in the water without deteriorating and souring the water. After much experimentation in a fish tank at home, he discovered the children's sweet called The Eternal Giant Psychedelic Gobstopper! This giant orb of confection was probably the sweet most feared by parents. Many mothers and fathers trying to get confectioners banned from selling them in case a child choked on one. Being 2 ½ inches in diameter, most children had to lick them down to gobstopping size, often becoming bored and tired of them before they got to a proper size to stop their gobs. It wasn't unusual to see a discarded glistening gobstopper of this size in the roadside kerb, festooned with black ants that too would become bored with the sweet but seemingly inedible ball. Bob noticed that the gobstoppers proved attractive to his little carp in his aquarium and that this particular sweet took over a year to dissolve, even with the persistent pecking from his little fish. Although the pioneers of the carp bait world were already using hard boiled egg based paste baits or boilies as they are affectionately known today, not all anglers were privy to them and so gobstoppers to Bob were the ultimate deterrent to small fish. Using the gobstopper as a hook bait which wouldn't impede the point of the hook proved to be a problem. However, Bob found that drilling the gobstopper through its centre with a drill bit just slightly smaller in diameter than the thickness of plastic mains wire sheathing, the gobstopper could be mounted on the length of the sheathing which was whipped to a size 2/0 O'Shaughnessy hook shank. Providing a not too hard cast was made, the gobstopper wouldn't fly off and stay on for a very long time. And all that before the Hair Rig too!

During an AGM in the close season of 1972 Bob Green struck a deal with the heads of the S.C.A.C. committee. He asked if he could pay a premium to the value of ten years club subscription to book swim Number 9 permanently (excepting the close season) until he caught Fatso. Bob said that he thought it would only take a couple of years to catch Fatso, and after that, he would leave the club to find waters new. The concept of getting ten years money pro forma paid into an angling club, which needed serious funding proved too irresistible. Bill Wilton, S.C.A.C. secretary of 30 years standing, agreed that the money would be welcomed as the club's leaky work party wooden boat needed replacing and a very light fibreglass replacement would be a boon to the already sore backs of keen close season work party volunteers. The deal was sealed and swim Number 9 had a signpost erected in it; the sign read:-

> **STRICTLY PRIVATE**
> **SWIM No. 9 RESERVED**
> **FOR THE SOLE PLEASURE**
> **OF BOB GREEN UNTIL FURTHER**
> **NOTICE!**
> **ANY ANGLER FOUND TRESSPASSING**
> **WILL BE DISCIPLINED BY THE**
> **S.C.A.C. COMMITTEE.**
> BILL WILTON - CLUB SECRETARY

Obviously, the typographical error 'Tresspassing' went unnoticed by most anglers, while others would tut and sigh at the clumsiness, but the message was clear to all! Maybe the extra S added emphasis. On the other hand, perhaps it meant that anyone who wore their hair long as they passed Greenie's Number 9 would get 'what for!'

This warning sign baffled quite a few passing anglers, none of them had realised that the S.C.A.C. had stocked Spigworth Pond with sole. Admittedly, while it is common for flounders to turn up in freshwater rivers, the welfare and longevity of these little flatfish became a great concern to club members. Concerned club members broached the subject in the next AGM, and suffered great laughter and ridicule!

Even though Bob's swim was officially exclusive, he decided that he would camp there throughout the season. Bob's wife Cecelia would cycle the 5 miles from their home once a week to bring him regular food and drink supplies, and let us be grown up about this – toilet paper! What goes in has to come out eventually, so to make his toiletry requirements complete, Bob bought a trench spade from an Army Surplus store. Although, the odd tube of toothpaste, bar of soap and a damn good wash would have been useful! Local farmer Jack Broughton's crops on the land around the perimeter of Spigworth Pond prospered well in certain spots for the next few years.

Bob remained in swim Number 9 without catching Fatso during the next two open seasons until mid morning March 14th 1974 when he tragically died from hyperthermia whilst listening to Tony Blackburn on BBC Radio 1 through the earphone of his Waltham transistor radio that he had purchased from F.W. Woolworth in 1971 for £1.49p. Tony Blackburn was playing the No. 1 hit single Seasons in the Sun by Terry Jacks when Bob peacefully passed away; only Bob would know that!

After a few days of the season closing, Bob had not returned home. His wife Cecelia became a bit concerned and decided to mount and ride her Raleigh Chopper bicycle up to Spigworth, despite the blizzard warning on the radio, to investigate. She found Bob there with his head bowed down and blankets wrapped around him, obviously dead!

Bob always said to Cecelia, that if he should die before her, he would like the funeral ceremony held at Spigworth Pond. The funeral ceremony was indeed held at Spigworth, and Landlord Charlie Chatswell arranged a lovely wake for all mourners at the public house called The Shepherd and Crook next to Spigworth Pond.

You may be wondering why still no angler fished 'Greenie's' Number 9? Bob Green's membership still had eight years left to run and as he hadn't caught Fatso yet his remains were allowed to remain there until his subscription had expired! Cecelia Green thought it would be a fitting gesture to allow Bob to see out his membership of the S.C.A.C. and then it would be time to inter Bob respectfully. Not only that, the lazy old git hadn't been to work for two years and it would take eight years to save up for the burial. In addition, there was a new three-piece suite to be bought for the lounge to replace the worn and tatty furniture that they'd had for over twenty years. Cecelia died three years later, when she was tragically knocked off her Raleigh Chopper by a milk float. S.C.A.C. secretary Bill Wilton conceded that it would be a good idea to bury Bob Green's remains under the banks of Spigworth Pond. He still lays there today under a wooden bench installed in memory of him behind Greenie's Number 9!

However, this was 1975, and Greenie's remains were still in swim Number 9; even though skeletal and his carp rods laced with spider webs. All passing anglers that knew Bob bowed their heads in respect as they passed his haunt.

A full hour had passed after Mark Gosling's fit of hysterical laughter. Squirt had been a bit worried about Mark after his face had turned purple and his lips blue, so he ran to the nearest telephone box to make a 999 call for an ambulance. This was in the day when you could find a telephone box without the fear of finding litter such as discarded Chinese takeaway containers, vomit, a bloodied bogey on a glass pane, or worse still, vandalized! The ambulance crew took Mark to Spinfield Hospital with a suspected heart attack, leaving Squirt to bailiff the anglers of Spigworth. This of course made little Peter Burt feel very important!

By 9:30pm, most anglers were set up for the night. Some were still trying to find a soft spot in the soil to spike their bank sticks and rod rests so that they didn't fall over with the weight of their rods and reels. The range of rods and reels was interesting too. There were Mitchell, Ryobi and Intrepid reels and Milbro, Hardy, Bruce and Walker, Gladding Sealey and Shakespeare rods. A few of the lower earners favoured Woolworth's Winfield range of fishing rods and reels. Good stuff for the money but Woolie's line was worth avoiding unless you particularly enjoyed losing fish!

The various styles of bite indication were also fascinating. Everyone was bottom fishing with lead weights, running ledger was the popular method, but a visual method of bite indication during the hours of darkness was needed. Torches weren't allowed to be used during the night except small shaded hand torches for tying hooks, baiting hooks, landing fish and unhooking them. So apart from holding the rod or line all night, which was impractical, a visual aid was employed to detect a fish picking up your hook bait. Wax tea light candles in jam jars to prevent the flame from being extinguished were popular and couldn't be classed as torches. The tea lights were used to illuminate a fold of aluminium baking foil dangling on a loop of line hanging between the reel and butt ring of the rod. When a fish took the bait, the foil would move with the line. This type of bite indication was very tiring and it would be common for a very work wearied angler to nod off and wake to find that a fish had taken his bait during his slumber and evaded capture. Some more serious anglers used electronic alarms for bite registration; The Heron based on Richard Walker's homemade buzzer called the Bedlam was a very popular bite alarm, although the sound it made was more like a squawk than a buzz. The Crow would have been a more fitting name. Fortunately, there were anglers who recognized that Heron's were annoying to listen to, and those with a bit of electronic engineering knowledge set about making nicer sounding buzzer boxes. Delkim and Les Bamford conversions became commercially available and one could send their existing Heron bite alarms off to these companies for conversion to make a nicer sound. It all made sense really. Why stay awake all night if you weren't catching anything? You could lie on a camp bed inside your Army Surplus bivouac and doze if the fish weren't all that interested; thus feeling fresher and more awake at dawn when a lot of the bite action could be expected. However, there was always a chance that you may catch a fish during the hours of darkness and the alarm would alert you, even if the buzzer did wake you up suddenly, not knowing where you were, felt dizzy, sick and feeling that you might fall into the pond because your legs were like jelly!

The range of baits used was quite ordinary in most cases. Maggots of all colours bought in the afternoon from the tackle shop and already stinking and frothing accompanied by ammonia fumes, bread flake, crust and paste, luncheon meat and sweetcorn being the most popular. One or two smarter anglers would use more sophisticated paste baits made from ingredients such as trout pellets; even hiding their trouty dough balls so as not to let other anglers in on their secret.

"Cor, you've had a few tench this morning mate! What bait did you use?" an inquisitive angler would ask.

"Maggits n' bread mate!" would be the answer from the soon to be 'Pinocchio nosed' tench angler. Interestingly enough, Badger Bill Parsons the Fred J Taylor freak, had a great deal of success using maggots and bread in conjunction for tench. His favourite bait presentation he named 'The Ballerina'. Badger impaled two white maggots on the bend of a size 8 Mustad Crystal hook; and wrapped a small flat piece of bread flake around the shank of the hook. Fishing with the bait only just touching the bottom, supported by a small porcupine quill float correctly balanced with lead shot, the bait presentation looked rather like a pair of sexy legs dancing under a frilly tutu. Badger had his idea published in the angling press, rumours and doubts about his sexuality spread far and wide and was forced to abstain from fishing for a month or so. When he returned later to wet his line he brought a bait which he thought was more masculine, lobworms! With two worms and a larger piece of flake mounted on a size 6 hook he reinvented the idea and called it the 'Dennis Law Rig' named after the Scottish footballer renowned for his famous 'Scissor Kick'! Surely, this rig would have re-established Badger as a macho angler. Not really, the bread flake still looked more like a tutu than a pair of football shorts and dear old Dennis's legs couldn't tangle up in the typical Karma Sutra performance as a couple of lobworms could. If Dennis's legs did perform such contortions, it would have made football look a bit shoddy! Therefore, Badger was condemned to be referred to as 'the pansy angler with the Mother's Pride loaf' for a little while longer; but a very successful pansy angler nonetheless.

Once all anglers had set up their tackle and self-promoted bailiff Squirt had pestered them to see that their permits and rod licences were in order just to make him feel important, the darkness descended upon them. From 10:45pm until midnight the anglers sat in silence in nighttime so black, you couldn't see your hand in front of your face. The timid night fishing virgins flicked on their hand torches every time they heard a noise in the bank side vegetation. When you're not familiar with the great outdoors during darkness, a dear little shrew rustling in the reeds can sound like a blood hungry panther about to attack you!

There are always cheats in fishing; some anglers set their watches a few minutes fast to get their first cast out. What the hell, they've waited for 3 months for this moment. 11:57pm is no sin surely!

*Sadly, during the October of the same season that Chris Moffat caught the 3oz 5 dram gudgeon, a pike angler caught the same fish and used it as live bait.

CHAPTER 2

JUNE 16TH 1975 DAWNS

It was 3:00am, and the first hint of daylight appeared in the still starlit sky. A windless cold 7 centigrade night was enjoyed and endured by the merry band of angling enthusiasts, completely oblivious to the notion that they were re-enacting the roles and instincts of many hunter gatherers in man's ancestry. The difference between these bedfellows and ancient man of course is that they don't catch fish to feed the family. It is purely the hooking, the playing, the landing, the touching and the pleasure of seeing a fish swim gently away into the depths, to sulk and probably make the same mistake a number of times before its caution sharpens. Yet, there will always be the odd angler every now and then that doesn't quite understand the logic of 'catch and return'. In the late 1960s, the S.C.A.C. welcomed a new member, Italian born Paolo Mancini. Paolo had gained British citizenship in 1957 and started his own ice cream business called Ice Cream Paolo, and was quite aware of the way to go about things in Britain. Unfairly, for some reason an unkind soul started a rumour that Paolo had been taking fish home to feed his family. It could have been a joke made by someone that was mistaken for a serious statement, but whatever, Paolo was under suspicion. The only fish Paolo had ever been seen taking home was an eel, which wasn't outlawed by the club rules and no offence to the angling club. Head Bailiff Mark Gosling watched Paolo like a hawk, sometimes through binoculars and sometimes through a bush in the swim next to the suspect. Then one day, when Paolo had packed up his tackle and heading home, he was stopped by Mark Gosling after little Peter 'Squirt' Burt had spotted some unusual movement in Paolo's canvas rucksack.

"There he is, there he is Mark, Mancini's pinching our fish!" Squirt excitedly pointed out to Mark Gosling. "Are you going to punch him Mark?"

"No, shut up Squirt, this has to be handled in a gentlemanly manner!" snarled Mark to Squirt.

Mark Gosling approached Paolo.

"Excuse me Mr Mancini; I'm going to have to ask you to open your rucksack so that I can see what you've got in there." Mark Gosling demanded.

"Well go on then." Paolo replied.

"What?" Mark asked.

"Ask me then?" said Paolo

"Can I look inside your rucksack Mr Mancini please?" retorted Mark Gosling with irritation.

"Why?" enquired Paolo.

"Because I have good reason to believe you are taking coarse fish that are the property of Spinfield Coarse Angling Club from this pond, to take home and eat!" said Mark Gosling with Head Bailiff Officialdom.

Paolo Mancini slid the straps of his rucksack from his shoulders, putting the rucksack down gently on the grass and said "Go on then?"

Mark unbuckled the many retaining buckles on the leather straps that held the canopy of Paolo's rucksack with a very self-important expression, but still with the miserable bastard look intact. Squirt stood behind Mark with both of his hands on his hips in a super hero stance, bubbling with excitement inside and a 'We've got you bang to rights mate!' smirk on his face. After the last buckle of the rucksack had been undone, Mark Gosling sharply lifted the rucksack's canopy to look inside. A rabbit leapt out of the bag over his shoulder and straight into Squirt's face, knocking the little creep off his feet and straight into 3 feet depth of Spigworth Pond water.

"Help! Help! I can't swim!" panicked Squirt.

"Well stand up then you pillock!" shouted Mark Gosling.

Mark Gosling apologised to Paolo for any embarrassment and inconvenience caused. Paolo explained that he had netted the rabbit early in the morning at the mouth of its warren to take home for a meal, but didn't want to kill it straight away as it was likely to be a warm day and he wanted to keep the bunny fresh. The bunny lived to hop another day, make more bunnies and with luck, avoid myxamatosis for the rest of its sweet short life. Soaking wet and justifiably humiliated, Squirt survived and irritated more anglers for years to come!

Still on the catch and release theme, during this era of Spigworth Pond you're reading about, there was a lot of confusion for anglers regarding the freshwater rod licence

Most coarse fishing clubs and societies requested that all member anglers returned all coarse fish except freshwater eels, alive to their residence after capture. However, on the reverse of the rod licences distributed by regional water authorities, there were guidelines for the legal size limits of coarse fish, e.g. Pike 18 inches. What did this all mean? There were one or two angling books published that told you how to catch coarse fish and gave recipe suggestions on how to cook them. It's quite obvious really, if you were fortunate enough to fish a pond or stretch of river that was owned by somebody that didn't give a toss for the welfare of the coarse fish, you could take them home to eat. These days it isn't unusual to see farmed mirror carp on the fishmonger's slab in supermarkets. Although it's most unlikely that these wonderful fish attract many shoppers to purchase them in place of a nice fillet of cod or haddock. Indeed, the very thought of eating such a thing as river cobbler from Vietnamese rivers may put a lot of wary fish fans off as one can't be certain of the pollution levels in the rivers of the Far East, unfamiliarity breeding suspicion and fear. Undoubtedly, it will be natural to eat coarse fish in years to come, although it is unlikely as I write in the early part of the 21st Century that we will see 'chub'n' chips' on the menu at the local chippy, for quite a while. I think that possibly the description of the platter would need a fair bit of tarting up to make it appealing in restaurants. Chavender et pomme frites would serve well as has the name huss or rock salmon been used to sell dogfish more successfully.

Back to Spigworth Pond, June 16th 1975 then! After a completely blank night for most anglers, except for the few that had disappointing and unwelcome tussles with slimy wriggling lengths of eel during the hours of darkness, the still early light of a June morning dawned. The mist of heat loss rose from the surface of the pond and the white periscope necks and heads of a Cob and Penn appeared just above the surface of the vapour, their little faun cygnets completely immersed and invisible in the upside down cloud. The dawn chorus of every local wild bird reaching its peak whilst rats plopped into the water to travel submerged in front of every angler occupied pitch, hoping that they were undetected by the strange bipeds that could possibly be their predators. The distant but unusually comforting sound of a lorry driven by an employee of a haulage company going long distance and meaning to get there on time. The fizz and whine of a hawk's wings cutting through the cold air as it plummeted to earth, to stun and kill a small rodent or bird. The flapping of a woodpigeon's wings as it took off clumsily from an English Oak tree. The reverberation of a mallard drake's quack, quack, quack from a far corner of the pond, the early morning Sun highlighting the melange of purples, greens and blues in the fine down on its head. And, the brutal noise of Graham 'Gruffer' Wheeldon breaking wind loudly and scaring a family of coots, disturbing the surface of the once still water and buggering up the delicate presentation of the perfectly cocked float. Gruffer though was a very proficient angler and had already started bagging up on good-sized roach and rudd in the 1 to 1 ¾ lb range, using small knobs of bread paste bait moulded around a size 14 crystal hook.

Gruffer Wheeldon was the kind of guy you wouldn't want to invite to tea at your mum's. Gruffer was banned from most public places, including The Shepherd and Crook pub adjacent to the pond. During a visit to this hostelry, the Mayor of Spinfield sampled a new local 4% proof ale called Spinfield Sparkler. Graham approached the Mayor who was posing with a pint pot for a photo shoot for The Spinfield Herald and said "Nice drop of stuff innit Mayor me old mucker?" whilst simultaneously releasing the noisiest, smelliest parp, completely clearing the pub of clientele and their dogs. "Plays 'avoc with me bowels though!" Graham assured the Mayor.

Pub proprietor Charlie Chatswell unconditionally barred Gruffer from the hostelry. However, not wishing to lose Gruffer's custom, Charlie agreed to a concession that he could drink outside. Gruffer also received Waitress service as part of the concession in case he accidentally let one go whilst buying a pint at the bar.

Many anglers were mildly envious of Gruffer's success on Spigworth Pond. Some anglers watched him through binoculars to see if Gruffer was doing anything radically different from everyone else. Some anglers crept up behind him to get a closer look. The only observation made was that just before Gruffer got a bite from a fish, he would blow off rather loudly. Could it be that the fish were attracted to a subsonic or even ultra sonic frequency resounding from Gruffer's flatulence? One radio news reporter and angler called Evan Wyatt even recorded Gruffer, gruffing away on his portable reporter's quality ITT cassette recorder, and a broadcast quality microphone secreted in the reeds around his swim. Evan captured a full side of an Agfa Gaevart C120 cassette of Gruffer's symphony, and rigged up an underwater speaker to play the posterior tunes to the fish. The results were inconclusive, and Evan noticed no discernible difference in his own catch rate. Evan's experiment concluded after just over 37 fishing hours when the cassette tape wrapped around the pinch wheel and capstan of his cassette recorder and snapped. C120s were annoyingly prone to this problem after too many plays. Obviously, Gruffer's habitual and socially unacceptable vulgarity had no affect, good or bad, whatsoever on the fish. It certainly seemed that Gruffer had very little problems with waterfowl and in particular swans disturbing his swim. Neither did he ever have issues with mosquitoes and gnats biting him, but that's probably an aromatic thing repelling the insects and something one can't emulate with mere audio reproduction. In addition, one thing that all of these mildly envious anglers overlooked, was that Gruffer may have been a better angler than them. But that's a typically testosterone driven competitive attitude that certain men seem to subscribe to.

While it is true that certain anglers are lucky and some seem to get the big one that everyone else has been after, it is more than just luck that brings an angler success and there is no substitute for experience and watercraft. To prove that fact, Walter Wigmore turned up with his son James on this beautiful and bright June 16th morning at 4:30am to show his son just how important those skills were. This was the first time Walter had been able to bring his eight-year-old son fishing. The excitement and fulfilment of having your little lad by your side, with the thought that he may in time take a shine to your favourite pass time and be a life long companion, is something that only a father can identify with. Well okay, after making that sexist statement as I write in the 21st Century, and before any lovely woman reading this leaps to the defence of the female of our species, I agree that this is also something a mother can feel with a daughter or even a son by her side. There are many woman anglers and a lot of them (yah boo sucks, it's not fair!) are better anglers than any man could ever hope to be, but in 1975 it wasn't common to see many fisherwomen on the banks of Spigworth Pond.

This wasn't the first time Walter Wigmore had taken any of his offspring fishing with him. Walter dragged his eldest son Stephen, now twelve years old, along seemingly every Saturday morning under complete duress until he was 10 years of age. Walter, a big Mr Crabtree fan had always enjoyed the ancient hunter fantasy of 'Me Crabtree, you Peter, we go catch fish now!' Truth to tell, poor old Walter was next to useless when it came to fishing, as his son Stephen often pointed out.

"We never seem to catch anything daddy. Are sure there are fish in here?" Stephen would ask Walter.

Alternatively he would ask, "Why does everyone else seem to catch fish and we don't?"

Walter's reply to that last question would be "Patience Stephen, the fish we are trying to catch are very special fish and not like the common types that other fishermen catch!"

However, in the October of 1973, things become all too much for little Stephen. Walter had his Mr Crabtree head on as usual and took Stephen spinning for perch on another S.C.A.C. club water called Brimbrook, in an attempt to hide his unsuccessful shame from the regular anglers of Spigworth. Brimbrook was a three-pond complex acquired by the club in 1968. The ponds were old red clay pits dug by a pottery and tile company called Fimble's Terracotta Limited. Fimble's allowed the three pits to fill with water fed from the nearby stream Brim Brook and made them available to rent for angling to the S.C.A.C in the late 1950s. Fimble's were having a bit of financial bother and needed a huge cash injection to save the company. In 1968, Fimble's offered to sell the ponds to the S.C.A.C. and the club applied for and obtained a mortgage to buy them. The club decided to name all three ponds after three famous eccentrics, Stanshall, Milligan and Dali. Stanshall was the smallest and possibly easiest to fish of the three ponds with a maximum depth of 5 feet when full. Milligan was the largest and deepest of the ponds with a depth at around 17 feet in certain areas with steep and sheer deep margins that were often 8 feet deep straight down in front of you. The last pond mentioned was Dali, which joined Milligan by a narrow finger, or causeway of water. From an aerial view, the two lakes looked like a pair of spectacles, the ponds being the lenses and the causeway being the bridge that connects the two lenses together. Dali was the pond that Walter chose to show his perch fishing skills off to their full glory to young Stephen. Walter's choice of armoury was a Hardy Bros. of Alnwick split cane Farcast spinning rod, coupled with a Silex Rex multiplying reel made by the same company. Walter pulled down the front of his Crabtree Trilby hat so that the brim shielded his eyes from the low Autumn Sun, he clenched his briar tobacco pipe between his pipe mouthpiece worn incisors and tutored son Stephen on the noble art of lure fishing.

"You see that stump sticking out of the water over the far bank Peter… err Stephen?" said Walter extracting the briar pipe from his teeth and pointing towards the stump with it.

"Yeah." said Stephen without the slightest tone of interest in his voice.

"Well that is the stanchion of an old jetty, and that's where I would expect a big old sergeant perch to be residing. The European perch or perca fluviatilis as it is known scientifically", explained Walter with a know it all swagger of his head, "loves to be waiting in ambush for some poor little fish to swim past."

"He's got dark olive and light green vertical stripes so that he can be camouflaged amongst the reeds and underwater vegetation hasn't he dad?" said Stephen with great knowledge.

"Yes, that's very good Peter…err Stephen, he does indeed." with a little uncontrolled excitement in his voice and a 'that's my boy!' tear in the eye.

"And he's got a spiny dorsal fin that he erects when in danger hasn't he dad?" said Stephen making Walter evermore proud.

"Yes, now, it's time to choose a lure from my lure box!" Walter said as he opened the lid of his wicker creel to pull out his lure box.

Walter opened his lure box, a converted El Pablo Havana cigar box that had a cork-based bottom to secure the lure treble hooks by spiking a point into the cork; this prevented a terrible tangle of very dangerous treble hooks. Stopping for a moment to rub a small palm of Dutch aromatic pipe tobacco called Troost, Walter stuffed the bowl, lit his pipe and allowed the sweet smoke to billow out, temporarily blinding his coughing and spluttering son Stephen.

"Now, this is what I think old Sergeant Perch would find enticing." Walter said as he unhooked a 2 ½ inch blue copper Devon minnow from its cork mounting.

"This little chap imitates a small fish as it spins in the water aided by these little propeller like fins, and is called a Devon Minnow." explained Walter to an already nodding off Stephen.

"Now pay attention Peter…err Stephen, watch and learn!" demanded Walter as he attached the swivel of the Devon minnow to the end of his fishing line with an unreliable Half Blood Knot. Walter confirmed that no one knows why there are so many knots with 'blood' in their names and that you can use Devon minnows anywhere in the world, not just in Devon, hoping that that would extinguish any silly or more importantly, difficult questions from Stephen.

"Before you cast to your quarry you must check that there are no overhanging tree branches above you that could snag the treble hooks of your Devon minnow." Walter demonstrated with melodrama as he looked all around and above him in a gyrating at the hip motion, almost making himself light headed.

Walter flicked his reel into free spool while braking the spool drum with his thumb, and pulled off 3 feet of spare line so the lure hung at that which he thought would be the correct amount of line between rod tip and lure for perfect casting.

"Dad, why do you call it a quarry when this is a pond?" enquired an inquisitive Stephen.

Walter explained that it was also a term used in hunting and fishing and that he didn't have time to discuss it right at that moment, more likely he didn't actually know himself and had only read the terminology in his old fishing books.

Walter demonstrated to Stephen the importance of casting. He pointed out that the cast would be overhead and aiming the rod in the direction of the old jetty stanchion.

"You see now Stephen, the important thing in casting is the timing of release. That is to say that when you lift your thumb from the drum of the reel it should be at exactly the correct time so your lure will follow through to its target."

Walter made his first cast and let go of the spool far too late, making the Devon minnow plop into the pond straight down in front of him.

"You see now Stephen, I did that on purpose just to let you see what happens when you let go of the spool too late." Walter lied.

Walter attempted a second cast and let go of the spool too early, sending the lure soaring up into the blue yonder and sending Stephen running for cover before it plummeted to earth.

"Was that to show what happens if you let go of the spool too soon dad?" enquired Stephen.

"Exactly!" said Walter with cringing pink tingling cheeks of severe embarrassment.

"Now this is how to cast correctly!" said Walter hiding his frustration.

Third time lucky and a perfect, well, almost perfect cast sent the Devon minnow to fall just to the left and behind the stanchion. Walter's multiplying reel's line was in a bit of tangle where he had allowed the spool to over run before braking it with his thumb. However, with the help of a darning needle Walter managed to untangle the bird's nest of line in a matter of moments, a quarter of an hour to be precise!

Once Walter had sorted his reel line out he continued to instruct Stephen on the finer art of spinning for perch.

"Now watch this Peter…err Stephen. What you do now is to imitate a wounded or dying tiddler by reeling the lure in erratically, constantly changing the speed of retrieve by cranking the reel handle at different speeds." Walter said completely forgetting where he had cast to and immediately snagging his Devon minnow on the rotting stanchion.

Realising immediately what had happened; Walter pretended that he had a biggun on the end of his line.

"Perch on!" said Walter hoping to eventually free the snagged lure by pulling on the rod at different angles and then declaring to Stephen that the blighter had got off after the hard fight.

"My, this is a big fish Stephen, I'm not entirely sure that it's a perch. It could well be esox lucius, otherwise known as the Northern pike originally from Scandinavia. In the times of Tudor reign, King Henry VIII commissioned the import of this wonderful fish as food for the banquet table around 1537 AD approximately...blah, blah, blah, drone drivel blah..." explained Walter to Stephen.

Stephen had already guessed that his dad didn't have a perch on at all and that the hook had snagged the stanchion, and being bored thought he'd grab a sandwich from his creel as he was also hungry.

"Now this little trick can ease the fish out of its stubbornness. Applying side strain by lowering the rod to one side of you and piling the pressure on can coax old Mr Pike into open water." said Walter, not even believing it himself.

Walter pulled so hard on the line, the split cane of his rod was creaking.

"Phew! If this fish isn't bigger than 20 lbs I'd be very surprised!" exclaimed Walter to Stephen, whose interest he'd now completely lost.

Stephen was still rummaging around in his creel searching for a tube of Smarties that he was sure he'd packed in there earlier.

Suddenly the unreliable Half Blood Knot that had been slowly undoing itself, lost its grip on the swivel of the Devon minnow and Walter's split cane spinning rod whipped back from its side strain – THWACK! - thrashing the back of shorts wearing Stephen's poor little bare legs. Stephen was none too impressed and a little bit weepy.

That was the last time that Walter had Stephen as a fishing companion, and it was the last time that Stephen wore shorts in public.

There was of course no reason to expect the Walter Wigmore's 'Mr Crabtree fishing experience' would be any different for his youngest son James... poor boy!

Of course, the 16th of June would not be complete without the wannabe match fishermen, with their giant tackle box seats rattling away with loose split shot and swim feeders. Walking uncomfortably with their giant rod holdalls full of rods that they probably wouldn't use in normal pleasure fishing, but have to lug it around for cosmetic and sartorial pomp. On this particular morning of June 16th 1975, Barney Tomkins arrived with his infernal bright blue, high impact plastic tackle box seat. With 20lbs in weight of groundbait, 5 pints of casters, 3 pints of psychedelic maggots, and a tub full of bloodworms. All because he read in a pre-season Angling Times with a free gift waggler float for the new season, that Fred Winkworth won a match on the River Naze with 63lbs of sticklebacks and bleak using the exact same combination of bait. Barney arrived at 8:00am with the intention of fishing until 10:00am because he had to put his car in for an MOT test for 11:00am that morning. Any angler worth his salt would know that the fishing would probably dry up once the summer sun became too high in the sky. Nevertheless, Barney didn't care about that because, being a very successful businessman with his finger on the pulse of point of sale stickers and cards for other businesses, he had the finest tackle money could buy, and the period between 8:00am and 10:00am was the most likely time for night fishing weary anglers to notice his array of posh kit. While most anglers practiced float fishing, Barney practiced gloat fishing. Barney was also a poor angler and no one cared about his expensive fishing tackle, people ignored him most of the time. We won't mention anymore about Barney, the boring twit!

By midday most anglers had gone home to get some sleep. Some phoned work to make some silly excuse about being ill and not feeling well enough to go in on that fine Monday morning. Most anglers went home with more inspiration to improve their techniques for the next fishing trip, some lied to their wives about fish that they never caught, just to justify the madness that is June the 16th. However, at midday you could guarantee to see a new member, sometimes a sea angler trying his hand at coarse fishing. He would turn up with his 12ft beachcaster, Intrepid Seastreak multiplier and bucket of King Rag, cast his 6oz Breakaway lead to the far bank rather than fish quietly in the margins on the opposite side and typically catch nothing. It was most unlikely that you would see him for much longer after that.

By 5:30pm June 16th the more serious anglers turned up to fish their favoured pitches knowing that most of the idiots would have gone home and burned out their enthusiasm for a few days, and you wouldn't have got any more serious than the carp anglers. This mysterious breed of angler that would almost risk divorce from their beautiful wives just to fulfil their desire to catch cyprinus carpio, take their pursuit very seriously. Some carp anglers have also lost their jobs and their homes because of their addiction to not just the catching of carp, but living the whole experience that is carp fishing.

Three carp angers, Will Spring, Jed Cleminson and Rick Western took their carp angling very seriously. All three men wore heavy make up and feminine clothes to ward off any of the usual 'caught anything mate?' anglers that would otherwise disturb their peace with idle chit chat and rubbish that no one was interested in. We have all had experiences at some point where we have felt that we wanted to tell these people to go away. One goes fishing to catch fish and be at one with the environment, not to hear about other anglers boastings of success on this bait or that. Well these three apparently camp carpers used this technique to full effect. Jed Cleminson always found 'Alright then sweetie?' very effective when he'd been approached by a boring swine on the bank. Rick Western liked to pout and show a bit of leg off. Will Spring sang 'See what the boys in the backroom will have, And tell them I'm having the same' in a rather convincing Marlene Dietrich tone, complete with shaven eyebrows. Needless to say when these three 'bank side angels' turned up at Spigworth for the night, they normally got most of the pond to themselves.

Even Will, Jed and Rick's tackle set up was a bit glam. They varnished and sealed their homemade Fibatube blank carp rod whippings with their favourite shades of nail polish. Experiments with homemade landing nets of various deniers failed, so they settled for material rather like fishnet stockings, but even in their fun way of deterring normal anglers, they were pioneers of landing nets, most commercial landing nets at that time weren't knotless!

Will, Jed and Rick proved to be a strange, even if miserable, fascination at one time for Mark Gosling, a bachelor in his Fifties. This made Peter 'Squirt' Burt quite jealous and hateful. Mark's fascination with the three men stopped after an altercation with Rick. In conversation with Mark, Rick just happened to say that he found that ginger haired children at school were often spiteful.

Mark said "Not all ginger haired people are spiteful!"

"I was merely saying darling, that it was my experience that ginger haired children at my school were a bit spiteful, possibly because they were bullied or ridiculed for the colour of their hair!" reasoned Rick.

"Well I'm ginger and I wasn't spiteful!" said Mark defending himself.

"No you're not, you've got white hair darling." said Rick.

"LOOK!" shouted Mark as he unzipped his fly and pulled the front of his underpants down to reveal a mane of very red pubic hair.

"Ooh I stand corrected poppet, whoops sorry sweetie!" Rick apologised as he lit up a St Moritz menthol cigarette.

"Yeah, right! So don't you go round saying that ginger people are spiteful or I'll smash your face in!" Mark threatened, and stormed off forgetting to zip up his fly, tripping as his trousers fell about his ankles.

At 9:15pm, after showing their S.C.A.C. permits to Squirt and asking about the well being of Mark Gosling who had been a victim of very severe indigestion and not the heart attack that everyone had feared, the boys got together for a serious chat about the night's fishing over a few Babychams before they settled down in their perfumed pitches. A little later, as the boys parted – B-E-E-E-E-P-P-P-P - a sound of a Bamford converted Heron bite alarm shrieked out in the dusk.

"Whose alarm is that?" said Rick.

"Not mine, I haven't even chucked in yet!" said Will.

"Me neither sweeties!" Jed confirmed.

The bite alarm was not going to stop unless someone picked up the rod and reel that the fish was rapidly pulling line from as it made a bid for freedom. There was obviously no one there.

Rick walked around the pond to find out whose rod the fish was on.

"I bet some idiot's left his line in the water while he's nipped into The Shepherd and Crook for a swift one!" said Rick with anger.

Rick located the swim that the alarm was shrieking from and nearly fell over backwards when he discovered exactly which swim the commotion was coming from.

"F-f-f-f-f-f-flippin' 'eck! It's Greenie's rod in swim number 9!" said Rick with disbelief.

Sure enough, a big-mouthed fish had picked up Greenie's bait The Eternal Giant Psychedelic Gobstopper, even after all that time in the water it was still on the hook.

Rick ploughed through the overgrown nettles that blocked Greenie's number 9 and grasped the carp rod that had its Garcia Mitchell 410 reel churning backwards with line stripping from its spool at an alarming rate. Striking the rod back, Rick felt a huge resistance on the end of the line. Greenie used to fish with the clutch of his reel spool clamped down tightly and only gave line to a hard fighting fish by back winding begrudgingly. Out of respect for Greenie, Rick played the fish in the same way. A full 30 minutes later, the fish was still fighting, but slowly weakening. Will asked Rick if he needed any help landing the fish, Rick thought it would be a good idea as light was fading fast and the last thing he wanted to do was to lose whatever was on the end of the line by fumbling around with a landing net. Eventually the fish began to give in and came in steadily.

Will flicked on a shaded hand torch and placed it in his mouth to see when the nose of the fish came towards the spreader block of Greenie's landing net. Just as Rick eased the fish towards the landing net, it made a last attempt dash towards the marginal reeds to the side of the swim, but the fish was all in, and entered the welcoming landing net almost lifeless on its side. Both Will and Rick saw a black spot on the head of the fish and gasped together "Fatso!"

Jed had been watching the proceedings and had already brought his camera and weighing scales with him. After unhooking Fatso the leather carp, Rick weighed her in the landing net and after deducting the weight of the wet landing net, she weighed in at 36lb 6oz. Jed clicked off nearly a full roll of 35mm film with his camera and flash as he photographed Rick holding Fatso whilst kneeling next to Bob Green's remains. It was probably one of the oddest photographs ever taken in carp fishing history, a glam angler with blue eye shadow and mascara holding a great leather carp next to a skeleton in a combat jacket and bush hat.

After returning Fatso to her watery home, the boys had another Babycham or two each and retired to their pitches for the night, not even caring whether they caught anything themselves. Fatso was a hard act to follow!

CHAPTER 3

WALTER CATCHES A BIG BASTARD

As most coarse anglers on Spigworth Pond had experienced, July could be a complete bunch of gonads for fishing. The days were often too warm and the nights took a long time to cool down. The carp and tench would find it the right time to make whoopee and were less likely to take bait, eels could become tiresomely catchable when you didn't want them, and the kids were on summer school holiday. Children on their summer school break, left to their own devices after their parents dropped them off during the week to get them out of their hair, or wigs, to fish all day and generally cause mayhem and disturbance to wildlife after they became bored with catching nothing. After the Tizer, pork pies, egg sandwiches and crisps had gone, there was nothing left for clueless junior anglers to do but throw things into the pond and at wildfowl.

However, not all parents leave their children to discover the great beauty of the piscatorial pursuit on their own.

Walter Wigmore was a wise and kind parent who took heart in introducing his offspring to the wonder that is coarse fishing. As previously mentioned, Walter's success was not remarkable in convincing his eldest son Stephen that angling was good fun. Nevertheless, Walter wanted to impress his youngest son James, and by God was he going to do it!

Walter and James arrived at Spigworth pond at 5:45am on a warm overcast Saturday morning. A little later than Walter had planned, James hadn't been to BIG toilets properly and Walter didn't want to resort to digging a hole in the field at the back of the pond with a trowel just to satisfy his little boy's toiletry comfort, he considered it a waste of jolly good fishing time!

On this occasion Spigworth Pond was oddly devoid of regular anglers, so Walter and James had the pick of any pitch they wished to fish.

Walter decided to fish swim number 10 as it shared the same patch of lily pads as Greenie's number 9. Bob Green's skeletal remains were still in residence at number 9, and many Spigworth anglers tried their hand at fishing the pads believing that the location was a hotspot for whoppers. The lily pads did have a sort of Crabtree feel about them. Badger Bill Parsons the Fred J Taylor freak, had a trouser full of big tench from number 10 with his Ballerina rig, so it did hold promise!

"Today James, we will be aiming to catch the shy and delicate but bold fighting tench, or tinca tinca as the species is known in the scientific world. The tench is identified by his powerful looking olive to dark green body with thick fins and a beautiful little red eye." Walter tutored James.

"What colour is the other eye then dad?" enquired mystified James.

With just a look of 'Don't be silly!' from his dad, James didn't dwell on the subject of tench eyes.

"The tench is also known as 'the doctor fish' because it is covered in thick mucus or slime and wounded fish that need a bit more slime to protect their skin rub themselves against him don't they daddy." said James with youthful wisdom.

"Well according to folklore at least James, though there is no real proof of that of course," replied Walter.

"When I have a cold and my nose is full of catarrh, that is mucus isn't it daddy?" asked James.

"Well yes, mucus of a sort James." Said Walter wondering where James's train of thought was going.

"So if my friend Timmy at school had a poorly knee after falling over in the playground and I wiped my nose on him; would that make me a doctor daddy?" James quizzed Walter.

"Well not really James, I don't think it would help very much at all!" said Walter abruptly, hoping that James would leave the subject of mucus alone and concentrate on the matter in hand.

The body of a floating beheaded coot slowly drifted by in the margins of Walter and James's swim. A common sight on Spigworth Pond and possibly caused by an attack from a mink. The nearest mink farm Fur Factors Limited was over 50 miles away from Spigworth, and the mink that dwelled near the pond were most likely generations down from the many mink released from their cages by animal rights campaigners with good intent. Unfortunately, as cruel as it is to breed animals purely for their pelts, mink possibly have no place in the ecology of the United Kingdom. What seems to be frenzied murder to many folk when they hear that 'Farmer Brown's chickens were savagely killed by a mink and left to rot', is most likely a mink doing what it has been programmed to do since its species evolved on this earth to create a food store. The only trouble being, that mink do not discriminate wild animals from livestock and the food store they leave behind isn't often retrieved later. In addition, of course foxes get a fair old bit bad press because of their taste for livestock as well. On Sunday mornings, one could hear the ridiculous parp of a hunting horn from the front car park of the Shepherd and Crook as the wealthy local hunt, reeking of sherry, on horseback in their red tunics, made their way to catch vulpes vulpes crucigera. The trip, trop, trip of the horse hooves and the squeals and yelps of the beagles demented with hunger, excitedly looking forward to a ripping time, and the hunts' firm belief that the hunt was doing this as a public service. Even in those days there were more foxes killed by motor vehicles than the hunt could ever control. It's a load of codswallop really isn't it?

Back to Walter and James Wigmore then...

Walter pointed out to some patches of tiny bubbles to James that were floating by the lily pads. The tench were already feeding. The sight of tench bubbles appearing on the surface has a strange effect on the senses of the tench angler. As the bubbles appear, it is almost as though one can hear them fizz as they break the surface tension of the water!

"Now James, I was originally going to throw in three walnut sized balls of ground bait. But as the tench are already feeding I don't wish to scare them, so I am going to gradually introduce small amounts of gentles so that they can find them as they probe around in the silt with their sensitive barbules." said Walter with know it all knowledge.

Walter took the lid off his plastic bait tub to reveal a writhing of hyperactive fly larvae.

"They look more like maggots than genitals to me dad!" said James with a puzzled look on his young face.

"No James, the name is gentles and is another name for maggots; I just like to use traditional words. Genitals are something quite different and something I will tell you about when you're a little bit older." explained Walter trying not to giggle.

Walter took a homemade catapult made from a forked branch of a tree, strong black rubber elastic and a hand sown leather pouch from his tackle box. Loading the little leather catapult pouch with a small amount of maggots, Walter gently drew back the catapult elastic and aimed towards the bubbly surface near the lily pads. As Walter let go of the catapult pouch, the maggots went everywhere, one somehow managed to fly backwards to end up in James's wide-open mouth. After a bit of retching and spitting, James composed himself and continued to enthuse in Walter's tench angling proficiency test.

Eventually Walter got the hang of using his homemade catapult, and gradually fed the tench with maggots, in addition feeding moorhens with the stray maggots that landed on the lily pads. With each pouch of maggots fired, the moorhens rushed about the green platters of maggots with lanky, skinny legs of panic and greed.

"Now I think that I've fed enough gentles into the swim to keep the tench interested James." said Walter as he set up a simple lift method rig on his rod.

Walter showed James how the lift method works "Now this simple rig is called the lift method and was used to great effect by Fred J Taylor to catch very shy feeding tench. Part of the problem with detecting bites from tench with usual float fishing techniques is that the fish can pick up the bait so gently that it doesn't always register on the float. With the lift method, the float is cocked by a single AAA split lead shot about 1 ½ inches from the hook and the bottom of the float is attached to the line with a single float rubber. The distance from the tip of the float to the lead shot is set to the exact depth of the water so that the tip of the float is only just visible."

Walter showed James how the float would behave when a tench picked the hookbait up, by lifting the float up and down with one hand and simultaneously lifting the hook and shot with the other hand.

Walter had made a number of floats from the quills of herring gull feathers, which he had trimmed so that they could barely support the weight of an AAA lead split shot by testing them for accurate buoyancy in a bucket of water at home. Being attached to the line by a single float rubber made from a small section of narrow rubber tubing meant that the float could break free should it become snagged in the lily pads. The quills were free and natural and couldn't be classed as anglers' litter.

"I will have to make a few dummy casts to set the float at the exact depth. I estimate the depth to be about three feet so I will slide the float up the line so that the tip of the float is about the same distance from the shot as the water depth." demonstrated Walter.

"There's no need for an overhead cast here as we will be fishing very close in, a simple underarm cast will suffice." said Walter completely unaware that the fishing line had looped around the tip ring of his rod.

"Gently swing the float and shot back and forth until you're happy that it's time to cast, this can also be used for precision casting to the edge of the lily pads." said Walter.

As Walter's confidence grew with the pendulum motion of the float and shot, he finally made his cast. With the line still looped around the rod tip, the shot swung back from the rod tip in a perfect arc to snag the hook in the brim of his Crabtree Trilby. After a few mumbled swear words such as 'damn' and 'blast', Walter managed to remove the hook from his hat without too much damage.

Walter made a second cast and was delighted to find that his estimation of the depth of water was spot on. However, he wished that he had put a couple of maggots on the hook as well. Walter's dilemma alleviated when he made another perfect cast to the same spot with a baited hook. Well done Walter!

For over an hour and a half the Wigmores sat with the patience of herons whilst the tench continued to bubble and cloud the water with silt, but without a single twitch on the float.

With both anglers feeling thirsty and after discovering that his thermos flask had broken, Walter sent young James off to Spigworth village's newsagent News, Baccy and Grub to by a couple of bottles of pop and some crisps. James made his way to the shop not far from the pond with a 50 pence piece feeling very wealthy. Two bottles of cherry fizz at 10p each and two packets of Golden Wonder at 5p each leaving 20p for change. Those were the days!

Walter sat mesmerized by the static float tip and drifted off into memories of his youth. He thought about his first true love Mildred Hargreaves, how she hurt his feelings when he saw her cuddling local Teddy Boy Cliff Screech behind the Spinfield Boys Club. How he got a thick lip from Cliff after picking a fight with him, and how Mildred laughed as Walter fell to the ground, landing in a filthy puddle. He remembered his first ever concert he went to see at the Spinfield Assembly Hall when a local band called Johnny's Jazzy Jivers played to an audience of over 100 people, and how he discovered after that evening, that he had developed a healthy loathing of Jazz music. How he hated eating cabbage and anything green and leafy but was forced to eat it at school by the dinner lady Mrs Windle - the heartless cow!

After further tortured thoughts, the herring gull quill float lifted slightly and settled. This roused Walter from his negative reverie, making him sit upright. The float lifted and settled down again, and again. Finally, the float rose up and settled flat on the surface of the pond, remaining there, leaving Walter unsure of what to do. After what seemed to be an eternity, the float slowly sank away and Walter lifted his fishing rod to an explosion of activity from a frightened and very angry tench. Lowering his rod, Walter applied some side strain to prevent his fishing line snagging on a lily pad. The clutch on the spool of Walter's fixed spool reel began to slip, giving out its clicking noise as the tench stripped line from it. Walter imagined that the tench was almost halfway into the underwater forest of umbilical lily pad stems. The tussle seemed to go on forever for Walter. It would seem like forever you see, because this, believe it or not, was the first big fish he had ever caught. Walter typifies the angler that does everything correctly but somehow manages to get it all wrong, seemingly always in the right place but at the wrong time.

More line stripped from Walter's reel as the tench gained more distance between them. The lily pads moved frantically on the surface of the pond as the tench fought to free itself. Walter decided to screw the clutch of his reel up tight, which was possibly something he should have done earlier. Walter could feel the vibration of his fishing line rubbing against the lily pad stalks, but the tench was tiring. Keeping the pressure on, Walter managed to coax the tench slowly towards the edge of the lily pads by pumping* with his rod and reel until the fish was finally out into open water. After a few more attempts to make for the lily pads, the tench finally rolled on its side and was ready for Walter's landing net. The tench was bigger than Walter could ever have imagined and he began to shake with excitement.

Lifting the landing net out of the water and gently placing the tench cradled inside onto the soft grass bank, Walter prepared to unhook his prize. Unfolding the net from the gasping fish, Walter observed that the hook had already dropped out of the tench's lip and snagged in the mesh of the landing net. Attempting to remove the hook from the net, the knot of the line tied to the hook parted. Luck was truly on Walter's side!

Walter weighed the tench inside a polythene carrier bag with his Little Samson spring balance. With his hands shaking so much, it was difficult to tell just how heavy the tench was. Finally, after Walter managed to steady his nerves, the spring balance settled on 5lb 2oz.

James had still to return with the fizzy and crisps, so Walter placed the tench inside his landing net in the margin of his swim. Walter filled his pipe with a generous wad of Troost and lit the pipe with still shaking hands. James would be so surprised when he saw what Walter had caught.

Puffing on his pipe and gradually calming down, Walter heard the metal gate to the entrance of Spigworth make its familiar clang as it closed.

"Mmm! Must be James." thought Walter.

Looking down at water in front of him, Walter noticed that his landing net was slowly slipping down in the water. Like a nightmare in slow motion, with Walter attempting to grab the landing net handle, the tench rose up in the water and slowly slipped away into the depths to sulk.

Walter felt like crying as he buried his face in his hands.

"Are you okay dad?" asked a worried James.

"You wouldn't believe me if I told you James." Walter replied with sadness.

"Everywhere looks wet around here dad. What's happened?" enquired James with a look of confusion on his little face.

"James...I have just caught and landed the biggest tench I've ever seen, it weighed 5lb 2oz and I tried to keep it in my landing net to show you but it slipped away while I was smoking my pipe. There is no one else fishing here this morning to witness my success and you probably don't believe me."

"I believe you dad; I've never seen you like this before! You must be very sad." said James in sympathy for his father.

"Yes I am very sad James, I feel that I have failed us." said a very woeful Walter.

"Let's try and catch another one Dad!" said a very positive James.

Walter never did catch another tench like that, but that didn't stop him trying.

*Pumping is the action of pulling a fishing rod back and reeling in line as you return the rod to its original position; thus gaining line and shortening the distance between angler and fish. Pumping is also a tern used by people with flat bicycle tyres!

CHAPTER 4

THE LUMINESCENT LADY

Every lake or pond has its resident ghost, and Spigworth Pond is no exception. Some ghosts are folklore, and some are fabricated stories designed to ward off unwanted young anglers from fishing at night, so other serious anglers may fish in peace. Some have gone to great lengths to reinforce the myths they have created by playing the part of a ghost and dressing in the traditional white bed sheet to frighten the unwanted anglers, often times scaring themselves as they woo and groan in the darkness. But these fake ghosts often get rumbled, resulting in 'darn you meddling kids, if my ghostly plan had worked I could have had the hole 12 acres of lake to myself', a la Scooby Doo!

As previously mentioned in chapter 2, by dressing in drag, Will Spring, Jed Cleminson and Rick Western have their own method of warding off unwanted anglers from fishing Spigworth.

It was a Wednesday early evening in mid August, and Will Spring, Jed Cleminson and Rick Western had already set up their gear and baited up to catch carp, their favourite species. Will and Rick felt the need to go home earlier and change their clothes after they had both arrived in the same silky blouses that they had purchased from British Home Stores the previous weekend. Mind you, at a sale price of £1.95. the blouses were an absolute bargain and totally irresistible! Will, Jed and Rick both agreed that they would phone and check with each other what they'd all be wearing so that this embarrassing situation would never occur again. Meanwhile, as Will and Rick were sorting out their sartorial elegance, Jed had to hide when his wife Winnie turned up at the pond in a vicious temper after discovering that he had borrowed her gold Lamé jacket that she wanted to wear on her night out with the girls to the Legs Inferno nightclub. It would be hard for anyone to believe that on Sunday mornings during the football season, these same glam anglers would be playing in a football match for Spinfield Wanderers, unshaven in manly soccer strip and without a single trace of Max Factor.

About 7:45pm, the figure of an unidentified angler on the far bank caught the attention of Will, Jed and Rick.

"Oh for goodness sake darlings, just when you think you've got the pond to yourself, someone else turns up to poop the party!" pouted Rick.

"Go over, chat him up and show a bit of leg off Rick?" Will suggested.

"No don't worry, I'll pop round and give him a bit of the Marlene, that'll get rid of him." said Jed.

"Probably will, knowing how bad your singing voice is poppet, woo hoo hoo!" Rick teased Jed.

Jed minced his way around the hard, sun-baked bank, risking a twisted ankle in his red stiletto shoes. By the time winter came, the bank's earth would be soft and stodgy and the high heels would have to be retired until the following summer. However, ever inventive, all three would be wearing bespoke thermal platform wellington boots made by the cobbler Whoops Sweetie! of Camden High Street.

Jed approached the unidentified angler to try to put him off staying the night.

"Hello love, you staying the night?" said Jed in a fey tone.

"Ooh! 'allo you! I like your shoes, your hairs nice too!" said the unidentified angler.

"My name's Cheryl by night and Charlie by day! What's yours hun?" asked Cheryl.

Jed's stance become more masculine and his voice became lower in pitch "My name's Jed, innit mate."

"Nice to meet you Jed, who are your other friends then?" Cheryl enquired.

"Um, that's Will and Rick and they're quite manly." asserted Jed

Taking his stilettos off, Jed ran back to Will and Rick and gasped "Flippin' eck it's a real tranny!"

"OH IS SHE!" said Will and Rick simultaneously in baritone tones, following that up with talking about football, very loudly in a blokey kind of way, and belching.

It's strange really, you'd think Jed would have cottoned on that the unidentified angler wasn't your ordinary blokey type of angler by the whiff of Chanel No5 that could be detected three swims away. However, this was a dilemma for Will, Jed and Rick; a genuine transvestite had beaten them at their own game. She had to go!

Some days later the three flustered camp carpers got together over four or five pints in The Shepherd and Crook and tried to work out a strategy to scare Cheryl off from the banks of Spigworth Pond.

"A ghost! A ghost, that's it, we'll fake a ghost!" Will said loudly as he leaned back on his stool and fell over backwards, forgetting it wasn't a chair.

They mail ordered some water based phosphorescent paint from a specialist paint company called Spooky Glow Juice, and set about painting a wedding dress and veil borrowed from Jed's old auntie Celia. After charging up with daylight or a powerful torch, the painted garment would glow for a couple of hours.

The plan was to take the flat bottomed punt from the angling club's boatshed and hide it in the reeds at the edge of the East bank woods. Pushing away from the reeds, Rick would punt the punt with a pole slowly as Jed stood upright in the vessel, like a glowing Boadicea in her chariot.

The nights could be Dylan Thomas's Bible Black on Spigworth Pond in those times, and with a waned moon, some nights were so dark you couldn't see your hands in front of your face. Light pollution wasn't often talked about and on a clear night the stars that were hundreds of light years away seemed so bright, it almost made them feel closer. How strange it is to be able to see the image of something that is most likely not there anymore! All this was to change twenty years later when Spinfield council installed streetlights along Long Farthing Road, the main road that connected Spigworth to the London Road junction at Randon roundabout. No Spigworth nights would ever be truly dark again.

It was time for Will, Jed and Rick to put their plan into action. Dusk on Friday August 22nd saw Jed dressing up in his auntie's luminescent wedding dress, undercover, in the woods that lined the East bank of Spigworth Pond. The wedding dress coated with phosphorescent paint, fully charged with daylight and topped up with a powerful torch, was stored in a lightproof sack to hide its luminosity until it was time to use it. Jed draped a black cloak around him to cover the wedding dress and veil, and quietly stepped into the punt. Rick sat in the punt behind Jed; there they would wait in the darkness until haunting time.

In the meantime, Will was having a bit of a chat about the fishing on Spigworth Pond to Cheryl who was already set up for the night, dressed in a fur hat and coat to keep him warm. Cheryl was there to catch the big roach that were more likely to make a mistake when darkness fell. Although no real competition, Will, Jed and Rick would still prefer that Cheryl wasn't there. In conversation, Will casually dropped in a comment about a spectral visitor called The Luminescent Lady of Spigworth, said to manifest herself at 10:30pm on August 22nd every year.

Cheryl didn't seem too phased, but the fear of uncertainty lurked inside him.

Will returned to his swim after wishing Cheryl 'good luck and tight lines', not completely sure whether he'd done a good job of spooking him or not.

It was 10:25pm, and a fox shrieked, baying for bunny blood in the dark distance. Jed stood up in the punt and took off the black cloak that had been concealing the glowing wedding dress, throwing the cloak onto the bank behind the reeds. Rick gently pushed the punt away through the reeds with a decisive but slow movement of the pole. Although with a bit of a wobbly start as Jed tried to balance himself, he looked extremely convincing. He was almost scared by his own his ghostly reflection in the water as Rick punted him close to the bank opposite to Cheryl. To reinforce his hoax, Jed started to moan in a way similar to how Donna

Summer would do a few months later with her hit song Love to Love You Baby.

Across the pond, Cheryl noticed this apparent apparition and lit up a long dark More cigarette calmly, and without a trace of fear. Cheryl immediately guessed that the three boys were trying to frighten him off the pond, and so he decided to enjoy the show.

What Jed and Rick didn't take into account was that Rick should have blackened his face and hands, his face illuminated by the glowing wedding dress made him very visible. Your average ghost was unlikely to need a punt or someone to punt to aid its haunting patrol!

It was difficult for Jed and Rick to know just how the performance was going for Cheryl, the little orange dot of Cheryl's smouldering cigarette end suggested that not an awful lot of fear was going on. Jed decided that they should turn the punt towards Cheryl and make it appear that the ghost was approaching him. This had to work, surely. Well, apparently not, in fact Cheryl started giggling, which progressed into hysterical laughter. Cheryl's laughter reverberating around the pond became an eerie heckling that was unsettling for both Jed and Rick. The cackling began to soften a bit as Cheryl's sides were splitting from much laughter. Suddenly, all present became aware of the sound of galloping horse hooves in the near distance.

The noise of the galloping became louder and slowed to a canter as the sound got nearer, the apparition of a bright white human head rose from the depths to hover above the water in the centre of the pond.

The head travelled towards the punt slowly rising to Jed's eyelevel, moving in as though to take a good look at him. With eyeless sockets and wide-open mouth, the head explored every inch of Jed's body as he stood there numb, unable to breath, speak or move.

With all the strength left inside, Jed managed to croak "Punt Rick, Punt?"

There was no response from Rick, he'd passed out as soon as he saw the spectre.

The head rotated 180 degrees and moved towards Cheryl who was also stricken with fear.

All Jed's muted senses came rushing back to him with such force that he fell out of the punt, thrashing about in the water. The surface of the pond glowed as the phosphorescent paint flooded out of the wedding dress.

Cheryl fled in a flap of fur coat and panic, leaving all his fishing tackle behind. The glowing head sunk back into the dark water of Spigworth Pond.

Will, who had dropped off to sleep after a hard day's work and a couple of bottles of Babycham, missed the whole spectacle.

The apparition which manifested itself to the night anglers was the Horseless Headman that was rumoured to haunt Spigworth Pond and the nearby woodland called Frapham Forest. Spigworth village Headman of the hunt, Richard Cartington, who had been having an affair with the then landlady of The Shepherd and Crook Daphne Billingshurst, met his maker in a grisly way on 22nd August 1908. Daphne's husband Wilbur was suspected to be responsible for stretching a snare wire between two trees in Frapham Forest with intent to decapitate Richard Cartington as he led the Spigworth foxhunt. There was no real proof as to who stretched the snare wire with intent to harm, but Wilbur received an unfair trial and was sentenced to the gallows to be hung until dead (I'm not certain that anyone has ever been hung until just before death, in law that is at least!)

Folklore has it that Richard's horse Wilhelmina bolted off after he'd been decapitated with his bum still in the saddle, disappearing forever, his head apparently catapulted into the pond as it was severed. It would seem that Richard Cartington has been trying to find his body and horse ever since he was murdered.

It goes without saying, that Jed, Rick Will, and indeed Cheryl, didn't fish Spigworth Pond at night for quite a while after that…the big wooses!

CHAPTER 5

SEPTEMBER

September, the days are still warm and everything still seems like summer, yet there are little hints of autumn being just around the corner. The Horse Chestnut tree drops its conkers, natural toys for children in the school playground. Children throw large sticks up into the branches to force the little brown inedible nuts down to the ground from the Horse Chestnut tree's selfish grasp. The conkers become trade items, a 99er swapped for a Woodbine. The cheating child strives to become 'conker king of the yard'. 'Soak 'em in vinegar!' or 'Bake 'em in the oven!' to make them harder. In addition, the lazy child that can't be bothered to get new conkers and uses last year's shrivelled up version, hoping that a bit of furniture polish will make it look like this year's conker.

When the sun goes down, the air gives a taste of autumn, just a slight nip in the air, but enough to make one put a jumper on when enjoying the country atmosphere.

Plants begin to show their age, with leaves turning brown. Blackberries, pregnant with juice, are enjoyed by many in a crumble or pie. The wild birds enjoy the blackberries, as many a housewife knows when she brings in the laundry to wash again, after discovering black and seeded bird mess streaking down her husband's white shirt.

Yes, there is a little sadness in saying goodbye to the summer, but for an angler it can be a wonderful time.

Fish seem to be easier to catch as the Sun's kiss becomes less warm on the water and their feeding spells seem prolonged. At this time of year the fish appear to be more beautiful having recovered from the cruel rigours of spawning.

September can make the less proficient anglers seem skilled, their dodgy old techniques beginning to work regardless of their tackle's crudity. At Spigworth, that was of course all less proficient anglers apart from Walter Wigmore.

Since Walter's tench victory in July, he had not caught very much at all apart from a few tree branches and his son James's ear. Eight years later, James would have his ears pierced, but this was far too early.

Walter also suffered some terrible heartbreak after reading a copy of Angling Times. Browsing through the weekly fishing paper, he saw a photo of his eldest son Stephen holding a magnificent perch of 3lbs 2oz. Stephen's friend Ian Screech invited him to go fishing with him and his father Cliff at Brimbrook. In the story underneath Stephen's photograph it read, 'Stephen said it was the best day's fishing he had ever had and he owes his success to the excellent tuition from his friend Ian Screech's father Cliff.'

Stephen had been secretly fishing with the Screeches for a considerable time, but was afraid to tell Walter for fear of upsetting him. It was upsetting enough for Walter to learn of Stephen's clandestine coarse fishing, but it was the horrid discovery that Cliff Screech taught Stephen to be a successful angler that really hurt.

"My Son, being taught fishing by that... TEDDY BOY!" thought Walter.

Cliff Screech apparently stole Walter's girlfriend Mildred Hargreaves, and now to add insult to injury, Cliff had stolen the right of a father to teach his own son how to fish, even if poorly.

Cliff and Mildred didn't tie the knot incidentally, Mildred chose to become a Nun, and Cliff joined the Royal Navy for 7 years.

Nonetheless, a September Saturday morning found Walter Wigmore and his son James trying their hands at roach fishing, or anything else that might be daft enough to pick up one of Walter's baits. All was serene until Peter 'Squirt' Burt walked around the banks of Spigworth pond with his pseudo angling club bailiff head on. In an S.C.A.C. newsletter, club secretary Bill Wilton mentioned a problem with the rise of non-members or poachers fishing the club waters, and that every member should ask unknown anglers to see their club permits if they thought they looked suspicious. Bill finished off his bulletin by saying 'You are all honorary bailiffs, let's wipe out this canker once and for all!' Making a grandiose statement such as that can only lead to trouble, much like a company boss giving every employee the title of 'Manager' believing that he'll get the best out of his team by making them feel special, i.e. Stationary Cupboard Manager, Tea Money Manager, Dustbin Emptying Manager and so on. Squirt had obviously taken Bill Wilton's statement too seriously, and with his usual vileness, went on a mission to catch the baddies.

Squirt approached Walter and James Wigmore and asked to see their permits. On seeing the name Wigmore, the nastier side of Squirt reared its ugly head.

"Ah, Walter Wigmore! Yes, we at the S.C.A.C. are considering awarding you with free membership for the next 10 years." said Squirt.

"Oh really? How very kind! Why?" asked Walter with surprise.

"Well on the basis that you never catch anything, you may as well not be here, and you're wasting your money!" grinned Squirt.

Unbeknown to Squirt, shielded by the bank side reeds, someone was fishing in the swim next to Walter.

"Oi! Squirt! Don't let me hear you talk to a fellow member of the S.C.A.C. like that again!" said a voice from the adjacent swim.

"Oh Mark, is that you?" whimpered Squirt.

"Yes it's me Squirt, and as Head Bailiff I would like to take this opportunity to remind you that you are not a bailiff, and as far as I'm concerned you never will be!"

"Well no, of course Mark, I was only checking permits after reading Bill Wilton's newsletter about the poachers and us all being honorary bailiffs." Squirt reasoned.

"You're not even an honorary human being let alone a bailiff. Now go away, stop annoying people and do something useful like fishing or keeping quiet!" said the extremely angry voice of Mark Gosling.

Squirt walked off crest fallen and occasionally looking back to see if Mark had thought better of his outburst. It wasn't being told off by his hero that hurt, it was the fact that he didn't even have the decency to come out from his swim to talk to him.

Well, the reason that Mark Gosling didn't come out from his swim was because it wasn't Mark at all. Richard Lucy, a long time member of the S.C.A.C. and competent angler, was also a voice impressionist, and a ventriloquist. Richard, who was fishing in the swim next to Walter Wigmore, was outraged at Squirt's bank side manner, and so he used his extracurricular talents to scare Squirt from hassling Walter any further.

Richard was such an excellent ventriloquist that he could make children believe that the fish he or they had caught were talking to them. Children would be fully engaged in conversation with a roach or rudd about television programmes such as Blue Peter or Paulus the Woodgnome. One day he was over enthusiastic with his impressions and ventriloquism, when he made Paulus's arch enemy Eucalypta the Witch's voice seem to emanate from the reeds, this frightened the children away. Bill Wilton the club secretary told Richard that although he believed that he only meant to make fishing more fun for the children, he should use his gift in a less frightening way. This time though Richard did intend to frighten someone away, and he felt that Squirt had gotten what he had deserved!

Unaccustomed to acts of kindness to him, Walter went around to the swim next to him to thank the mystery voice for his benevolence. Richard told him that he was welcome and he would defend anyone from people who inflict cruelty on the less fortunate.

"Anyway, my name is Richard and I'm pleased to meet you." said Richard, as he offered the hand of friendship to Walter.

"Have you caught very much this morning Richard?" enquired Walter.

"I've had a few little roach, but nothing else." replied Richard.

"Well that's a lot better than I have fared, I never seem to catch very much." Walter said with his head bowed in shame.

"There are a lot of anglers who have similar misfortune to you, I can't think why really. Everyone seems to be doing the same thing roughly, and yet some fare better than others do. I suppose luck has something to do with it, but you do also have to be in the right place at the right time." reasoned Richard.

"I think that I'm always in the right place and at the right time. Moreover, I'm certain that if another angler was fishing in the same spot with me, they would catch fish and I wouldn't!" proclaimed Walter.

"Mmm...a bit like the lucky blighter who plays fruit machines and wins the jackpot regularly I suppose?" concluded Richard.

"Exactly!" nodded Walter.

It must become quite irritating for all the people who fill up the fruit machines without gain, prior to the lucky punters putting a coin in the slot, and then the pennies falling from heaven. Ugh, that most awful noise of coin clattering success!

Many unlucky anglers give up after a while, believing that they are just wasting their time. In contrast, Walter had the dogged belief that he would one day catch many fish, and the quality that he did share with successful anglers was that he was patient.

Apart from luck, skill, patience, good bait and tackle, quietness and concealment are useful tools for success in fishing. As one of the books by author Denys James Watkins-Pitchford's* title suggests 'Be Quiet and Go A-Angling.' Quietness is not just limited to the voice though, as any angler whom has experienced a buffoon up the bank merrily bashing his umbrella spike with a mallet into rock hard earth can qualify. Indeed, fish can detect footfalls. Many a small stream chub angler will know of times when they have been as stealthy as possible in pursuit of their quarry, and then a crack of a twig hidden in the vegetation underfoot has sent the fish disappearing into the safety of an overhanging bush.

Concealment is another thing entirely, if you have made yourself as inconspicuous as possible by being quiet, you may as well try to be as invisible as possible too!

It is no use being quiet if you are easily seen by wary fish, keeping as low as possible can help to make you less visible to the fish.

The choice of clothing is also important for many anglers. It's often advised in angling literature to dress drably to blend into the background. It isn't clear whether the colour of clothing an angler wishes to wear will influence his success in fishing, or how fish would react to an angler wearing a fluorescent orange Flamenco shirt and bright blue sombrero. Needless to say, wearing brightly coloured clothes should be avoided when angling as it can look unsightly and does not fit in with the environment, although a sombrero may be pressed into use as an emergency umbrella. Regarding sombreros, it is advisable not to use tent pegs and guy ropes to prevent them from blowing away on windy days. It is easy to forget that your sombrero is tethered to the ground during the excitement of catching a big fish, if you stand up suddenly to play the fish you could possibly pull the hat over your eyes, and in the worse case scenario, suffocation could occur! A sizeable hatpin will suffice, but be careful, they can be very sharp!

The master of concealment was S.C.A.C. member Ian 'Camou' Lake. Ian spent an awful lot of time and money in Army Surplus stores in the name of concealment. Everything Ian wore was camouflage, he painted his rods and reels with a camouflage pattern and smeared his face with green greasepaint to mask his features from the fish. Ian had a different approach for night fishing and had a change of black clothing and boot blacking for his face; he also had a terrible complexion. When he had caught a notable fish, he jotted down the weight and length of the fish, weather conditions, air temperature and time of day or night – with a camouflaged pen in a camouflage pattern covered notebook.

All the regular anglers enjoyed teasing Ian about his camouflage attire. If Ian joined in on a conversation, some wag would say 'Who said that? Oh it's you Ian I couldn't see you as you were so well camouflaged!'

A close season work party became a search party after Ian had dropped his camouflaged pen on the grass. Eventually Mark Gosling found the pen by treading on it; the crack of the pen's plastic barrel snapping revealed its location. Ian learned from this experience and made himself busy by buying a budget price pack of biros from F W Woolworth and painting them with enamel paint in camouflaged patterns.

There was still enough foliage around the pond in September, so Ian was still able to approach his quarry with commando stealth. Ian's quarry was the common bream, and any bream that came was welcome, although he secretly wanted to catch one of the few huge bream that swam the depths of Spigworth Pond. When a bream is big, it really looks big, and one bream regularly spoken of but not often caught was Brutus. Brutus was reputed to be nearly 20 years of age.

Ian had been baiting his swim up with a 1-gallon bucket of mashed bread on the previous night and things were looking good as streams of bubbles decorated the surface of the pond. Swallows skimmed the water's surface breaking the bubbles as they took one of their last drinks before they made their return flight to South Africa.

Using a simple running link ledger with two swan shots and a size 8 crystal bend hook baited with a bunch of brandlings that he'd obtained by turning cowpats over (the filthy beast), Ian was already getting bites registering on his swing-tip. The bream swimming into the fishing line made most of the indications on Ian's swing-tip. Although line bites are frustrating, making the angler tense as the swing-tip rises and falls, there is no mistake when a bream does eventually take the bait.

Having travelled to Spigworth Pond by bus, pensioner Laurie Bluet, one of the original S.C.A.C. members, was setting up his tackle for a spot of peaceful fishing, also to get away from his nagging wife of 31 years for a few hours or so. To be fair Laurie, or 'Antique Bluey' as other anglers referred to him behind his back, did need a fair bit of nagging because he had the dynamics of a sloth when it came to performing simple domestic chores. His wife Dorothy's nickname for him was 'Slow Loris'. The anglers called him Antique Bluey because of his choice of tackle. His rod, made of greenheart, he coupled with a small wooden Nottingham reel, both of which were hand me downs from his father. Greenheart, although very heavy, was a popular choice of wood for rod makers as it was very strong and didn't break easily when bent. Every close season would see Laurie stripping his rod down, removing the rod rings, rubbing the old varnish off and re-whipping the rod rings on with silk thread, sealing the whipping with cellulose dope and finally re-varnishing the rod for the new season. All the hard work that Laurie put into renovating his rod completely baffled Dorothy, as it was so uncharacteristic of him.

"If you put as much effort into keeping the shed tidy as you do with renovating your rod I wouldn't mind!" Dorothy would say.

"Oh leave orf you old bat!" Laurie would reply lovingly.

The only modern item in Laurie's kit was the nylon monofilament line, but that was only because he was forced to buy it because he couldn't buy the old line that was originally on his hand me down reel. He made his own floats from crow's quills, porcupine quills, balsa wood or cork. Laurie was indeed still living in pre Mr Crabtree land. Even Bernard Venables had updated his cartoon strip fishing character by then thank goodness, the carp fishing piece with the 1X cast threaded through a par boiled potato, secured by a treble hook had to go!

Fish of course are completely unaware of the antiquity or the newness of an angler's fishing tackle, in fact, and most unlikely the first thing on their minds when they pick up the wrong piece of food and the whole world goes crazy as they are pulled in a direction they don't want to go. By this token, Laurie Bluet stood as good a chance as any angler did as long as he had his bait presentation right. Unfortunately, Laurie's casting couldn't be classed as perfect and it wasn't uncommon to see the trees above his swim to be festooned with crow or porcupine quill floats.

In addition to being a pensioner, Laurie suffered from acute myopia. Laurie's ultra thick lens glasses caused him a spot of bother occasionally. When engaged in conversation with anyone, he would as a force of habit, take off his glasses to speak. Whether the removal of his spectacles helped him concentrate in conversation was unclear, but Laurie almost set himself on fire when one of his spectacle lenses focused a pinpoint of searing Sunlight on one of his canvas bumper boots. As the smoke began to billow from his boots, Laurie thankfully had the good sense to jump into the pond to extinguish himself.

Laurie, now ready to tackle the piscatorial delights that swim in Spigworth Pond, threw in a handful of groundbait to cajole fish of any sort to feed in his swim. His groundbait was a blend of 2lbs of breadcrumb, a tablespoon of mixed spice stolen from Dorothy's spice rack, a wee sprinkle of sage and onion PAXO, 2 teaspoons of Pernod and minced up leftovers from Dorothy's stale fruitcake. What fish could resist such culinary treats?

The wind was starting to pick up as it often does in the morning after a completely still night. Laurie sensibly decided to fish with a free running ledger without a stop shot behind. The stop shot is designed to prevent the lead Arlesey Bomb from running all the way back up the fishing line; however, Laurie chose to omit this important detail. By Ledgering, Laurie's hook was less likely to snag on the trees above him with a shorter length of line dangling from the rod tip when casting.

'Plop!' In went Laurie's first overhead cast, the Arlesey Bomb arriving dead on target. Unfortunately, Laurie was completely oblivious that his hook had still snagged on a willow branch above him regardless of the measures he had taken to prevent that from happening. With the Arlesey Bomb able to run freely, a straight taught line angled out of the water between bomb and tree.

"Still trying to catch those sparrows then Laurie?" said a voice from behind.

The voice was that of the real Mark Gosling, he was walking the bank on bailiff duty.

"Eh? Oh hallo Mark, I haven't seen you for a while." said Laurie.

"No, I haven't been fishing very much this season since I was taken to hospital with a suspected heart attack." explained Mark.

"Is everything alright?" enquired Laurie.

"I think so, it was severe indigestion, but the doctor is a bit worried about my weight and he's told me to give up the pork pies and sausage rolls." said Mark as he wobbled his large belly with his hands.

"Do you want me to untangle your line from the tree Laurie?" offered Mark.

"Eh? Who put that up there?" puzzled Laurie.

"I don't know, maybe it was the hook fairy." said Mark with his characteristic miserable bastard expression.

After giving Laurie a few tips on how to cast underarm, Laurie went off to check more permits before trying a spot of fishing himself.

Ian 'Camou' Lake had been getting a quite a bit of action, but was being pestered by 'nuisance' carp and tench. Walter Wigmore found it strange that anyone could become annoyed when these wonderful fish graced their fishing line. However, Ian considered himself a specimen hunter and any fish apart from the species he wanted to catch, however hard fighting or beautiful that fish may be, was a time wasting nuisance.

To a non-angler this may seem ungrateful, but no one but a specimen hunter can understand the frustration of latching onto a an unwanted fish after casting a well presented bait intended for a certain species. Anglers are weird, and specimen hunters take their weirdness to a different level.

Little James Wigmore had started getting a few bites while his dad Walter was having a bit of a natter with ventriloquist and impersonator Richard Lucy.

"Dad, Dad, I've got one!" shrieked James with underpants wetting excitement.

Trying to hide his excitement, Walter casually walked back to his swim to find James with a little perch dangling from his rod. The pretty little perch with its large spiny dorsal fin and its alternating dark and light green vertical stripes is often times the very first fish a young angler will catch, and of all the fish that angler catches in years to come, that little perch will never be forgotten.

"That's wonderful James!" said Walter in congratulation.

"Can I keep him and put him in the pond in our garden please?" asked James with childish yearning.

"Um, well, I'm sad to say it isn't really allowed James, you'll have to put him back." said Walter with a pang of sadness for his boy.

At this particular point, Mark Gosling was walking past and saw James with his bottom lip stiffening and his eyes filling with tears.

"Oh that's a nice perch matey!" Mark said to James.

"Yes it's a perch!" said James with a gentle sob.

Mark looked at Walter and told him to unhook the perch, put it inside James's landing net and place the net in the margins so that it can swim around in it.

"I'll be back in a minute." said Mark as he walked off to the boat shed.

Inside the angling club's spider-infested boatshed, was years of junk that had amassed over the fishing seasons since the 1950s. On a shelf at the back of the shed was a large glass catering jar that used to bear the label Horlicks. This gargantuan glass vessel was once the property of a small faction of anglers called The Night Owls Fellowship. This little clique of anglers fished only at night and slept by day. They all worked the night shift in the large local pharmaceutical manufacturer called Brougham's. After a night's fishing, all the Night Owls often found it hard to sleep when they got home, so it became a habit to have a nice hot mug of Horlicks before going home to bed. This was rather the reverse of someone partaking of morning coffee to wake them up.

Therefore, this legacy from the Night Owls had been in the boatshed ever since they finished their last hot steaming mugs of malty goodness.

Mark Gosling took the glass jar from the shelf and blew the dust off, this made him convulse into a fit of wet sneezes.

Having made the glass jar look reasonably clean, Mark took the jar to the patiently waiting James Wigmore.

Mark filled the jar with pond water and asked James to place his little perch that had been swimming about in his landing net, into the jar.

"There you go matey, you can watch him swim around in there before you put him back when it's time to go home!" said Mark with an unusually friendly appearance to his face.

"Can I take him home please Mr Gosling?" begged James.

Mark looked at Walter Wigmore who was wearing an 'I don't know, it's up to you.' expression.

Mark explained, "Well the thing is matey, if you took him home to put in a tank or in your garden pond he would be very lonely, and that wouldn't be very kind."

"What if I caught him a friend to take home with me as well?" asked James.

Mark rubbed his unshaven chin with the palm of his right hand and paused for thought.

"If you catch his friend, and it must be his friend, because I will know if it is his friend or not, then you can take him home!" bargained Mark.

There were millions of little perch in Spigworth Pond despite the devastating 'perch ulcer' disease in the early 1970s, which virtually wiped this species out in some areas, so two taken from the pond would not have made very much difference.

Walter Wigmore relaxed and bathed in his son James' victory, hoping that he was going to catch another little perch.

Things were still plodding along nicely for Ian Lake with twelve reasonable sized bream gracing his landing net, none of them however were anywhere near the size of Brutus. Meanwhile Antique Bluey had caught a few nice sized rudd, a few more trees and a barbed wire fence.

It was nearly midday and the clouds were gathering to hide the sun. At this time of year though on Spigworth, the fish could bite all day long.

Pike were swirling and attacking shoals of young fish and heaven forbid any young moorhen that bobbed past their lairs. What a sickening sight that is, seeing a little sweet black ball of fluff performing its own version of swimming, suddenly engulfed in a cruel vortex of hunger. 'It is only nature!' the wildlife experts say, and it is with that self same sentiment that the professional wildlife experts willingly watch and film an animal being hunted down by a big cat. Somewhere inside some of us, there is a feeling that somehow this is wrong.

Watching this display of predatory menace was keen pike angler Rob Wansford, who in a few weeks, would be whipping out his Jardine Snap Tackle and Pike Gag, and with a bit of luck haul out a monster or two. The pike in Spigworth were generally average in size, but there were reports that one or two may be over 25lbs, and this made it worth trying one's luck.

A Pike Gag incidentally is not a joke about pike fishing, it is a piece of equipment! Young pike anglers of the 21st Century may not have ever owned a Pike Gag or even seen one. This barbaric piece of spring-loaded equipment was invented to keep a pike's mouth open whilst unhooking a set of treble hooks, to save one from getting their hand trapped in the cavern of backwardly pointing needle sharp teeth. Unfortunately, the gag could at times break the jaw of the pike, and so the fish would probably not have been able to feed properly afterwards, consequently death through starvation could follow. Today's pike angler unhooks the pike by rolling the fish over on its back on a padded mat and straddling the fish between two legs to prevent it from thrashing about and harming itself. By opening the fish's mouth under the chin where the gill cover openings start with two fingers of one hand, he is able to remove the hooks with a long pair of artery forceps. This exercise is best carried out wearing a thorn proof gauntlet as even the gill cover openings can be very sharp.

Rob Wansford would have to wait until October 1st before he could fish for his favourite species. It was tradition and a club rule to only fish for pike from the beginning of October until March 14th.

Having lost most of his tackle in the trees, Antique Bluey decided to call it a day, pack what was left of his tackle away and leave for home. It was twenty minutes to two and with a bit of luck he would be able to catch the two o' clock bus home, and with luck, he'd be home in time to catch a bit of World of Sport with Dickie Davis. Saturday night was his wife Dorothy's steak and kidney pudding with pease pudding night, with lashings of brown sauce and a couple of bottles of brown ale, it would more than make up for yet another disastrous day in the Laurie Bluet catalogue of angling disasters.

Ian Lake was still plugging away and catching just about every species except bream, this was testing his patience to its limits.

Little James Wigmore was getting many bites but missing all of them; so far his little perch's friend was proving elusive. His father Walter was trying to impress on him the benefit of concentrating on the float and striking his rod to set the hook rather than reeling in and hoping the fish was still on the end. It was tiring work for any small boy to concentrate for so long, and James was getting very weary.

Then suddenly, James float slowly slipped away into the depths of Spigworth Pond. "Now lift your fishing rod up quickly James, but not too quick, because if it's your little perch's friend he will fly out of the water and past your ear." Walter instructed James.

As James lifted his rod, he felt a solid thumping on the end and a brief flash of bronze scales appeared in the water.

"Steady now James, if my expert fish identification skills are up to scratch, you have a very large common bream on the end of your line." Walter said with great pride.

Walter carried on with his educational advice, "The common bream or abramis brama as the species name is called in Greek, can grow to a great size and it is not uncommon for them to grow over 6lbs."

James wasn't listening and his only thought was how he was going to land this hulking great thing in his little landing net.

"I say, does anyone have a large landing net my little son can use to land this leviathan of a common bream please?" Walter asked loudly.

Ian Lake reeled his tackle in and excitedly ran to the Wigmore's pitch with his landing net.

"My arm is beginning to hurt Daddy!" James complained.

"It's alright, the fish is almost tired and we'll soon have him in the net." said Ian Lake calmly.

No sooner had Ian made that statement, the bream came to the surface, rolling on its side, ready to slide over his landing net.

"Crikey, it's Brutus!" gasped Ian.

As Ian lifted the landing net out of the water, he knew it was going to weigh over 7lbs. Ian weighed Brutus in a specially made weighing sack; the weighing scales settled on 7lbs 6oz.

"7lbs 6oz James, what a whopper, I am so proud of you son!" Walter congratulated James.

"Yes James, very well done to you little chap!" Ian agreed sportingly.

After having his photograph taken holding Brutus by Ian with his Polaroid Instant Camera, James, with the help of his dad, returned the big bream to its watery home.

Watching the bream swim away, James remembered his little perch in the big glass jar. Feeling replete in his angling experience for the day, James gently scooped the little striped fish out of the jar with his hand and returned it to the acres of Spigworth Pond, knowing that he had done the right thing.

James slept well that night, holding the photo of Brutus in his little hand.

*It is no great wonder that Denys James Watkins-Pitchford used a pen name of Michael Traherne and finally BB after trying to say that mouthful!

CHAPTER 6

THE IMPORTANT PIKE MATCH

It was the evening of Wednesday October the 1st 1975, and glum faces were abounding in The Shepherd and Crook. Pub proprietor Charlie Chatswell was the bearer of sad news to the local clientele of his hostelry. Another regular customer, Antique Bluey, had passed away suddenly while he was working in his garden on the previous Sunday.

Laurie Bluet's poor widow Dorothy had been ill with grief and rushed by ambulance to the Cardiac Ward at Spinfield General Hospital, everyone who knew the Bluets were very worried.

This terrible news affected Charlie Chatswell deeply, so much so that his usual 'happy-go-lucky' exterior wasn't surfacing.

Charlie had barred a not so regular customer for mocking the new hanging pub sign. Charlie commissioned a renowned Shropshire sign maker and artist, Aubrey Stephens, to make a new sign to replace the thirty-year-old one that was badly worn, defaced and peppered with shotgun pellets. It was a simple instruction over the telephone, a hanging pub sign, 36 x 28 inches, and the name of the pub is The Shepherd and Crook. Therefore, a nice representation of a Shepherd holding his crook, and possible a dear little lamb under his arm, should have been easy to depict, one might think. Well, you would think so wouldn't you? Unfortunately, when the sign arrived for hanging, Charlie was away for the day, sampling some guest ales.

When he returned from his important business appointment, even if he had slightly over indulged, Charlie was enraged when he saw the new sign. A visual representation of a shepherd gripping a man wearing a flat cap, bandit mask and a black and white striped jersey by the scruff of his neck was not what one would expect. Charlie demanded that the sign fitters put the old sign back up until a decent replacement with the correct depiction was available. Sadly, this was not possible, as the men who had fitted the new one had trashed the original. Therefore, the sign, no matter how embarrassing it was, had to stay until the correct version arrived.

Charlie would usually take all this silliness in his stride, but having knowledge of the terrible news of Bluey and his gravely ill widow, he was not going to suffer fools lightly. Mocking the pub sign was the last straw for Charlie, so he kicked the joker out of his pub!

Not many people knew that Laurie and Dorothy were self-sufficient. Apart from their pension payments, all extra money they earned came from the sale of the vegetables that Laurie expertly grew in his garden and green house. Rabbits and pigeons that Laurie would eagerly go out to shoot, often supplemented their meat. Consequently, the old couple didn't have a great deal of savings; Dorothy would not be able to afford a decent burial for Laurie.

"If we all chipped in I don't think we'd raise enough cash to give Laurie a good burial, and I don't like the idea of him being interred in a pauper's coffin." said Charlie with a pained expression.

All present at the bar racked their brains, trying to think of ways to raise enough money for Laurie's funeral.

A raffle draw was the first idea, although as Charlie quite rightly pointed out, it was hard enough getting customers to stump up for the meat raffle tickets on Sundays. No, there had to be something else.

Pike angling enthusiast Robert Wansford listened to the fund raising ideas and decided to put his two pennies worth in, "What about a sponsored pike match?"

"Eh?" said Charlie.

"It's officially the pike season now and what better way of raising money is there, than pike anglers being sponsored to catch their favourite species." said Robert.

"That's not a bad idea, not a bad idea at all!" said Charlie excitedly.

"Yep, well I can get at least 15 anglers interested in participating, if the word gets about we could end up with more, I'll get some flyers printed too." Robert asserted.

Robert Wansford telephoned his friends, and they in turn helped by putting the feelers out for more anglers.

The only problem was that Laurie's funeral was likely to be within a week and it was doubtful they could get enough sponsorship before then.

"Who's going to arrange the funeral while Dorothy is in hospital then?" queried local butcher and regular customer Ronnie Smith.

"Ooh, good point Ronnie, the thought hadn't even occurred to me." said Charlie.

Charlie decided that he would make the arrangements because Laurie and Dorothy hadn't any immediate family that he knew of. He also made the decision that he would take care of the payment regarding fees for the funeral directors etcetera. Charlie would pay for everything in advance, and the sponsored pike match could take place sometime after to allow sponsorship money to accrue. However much sponsorship money was raised would be paid back to Charlie, and if it didn't quite make up the amount of the funeral costs, the balance would be Charlie's contribution. Immediately after the adverts were printed, the 'Bluey Pike Match Street Team' pasted or pinned flyers to almost every upright construction to announce the sponsored pike match in the village of Spigworth and a few neighbouring villages.

Robert Wansford also paid to place a little advert for the following Wednesday in the small ads section of a weekly angling publication to drum up more sponsorship. Although the advert didn't attract any sponsorship, it did receive a fair amount of attention, despite the short notice. Robert received telephone calls from anglers from various clubs asking if they could participate. This could be difficult because the venue for the pike match was to be Spigworth and only supposed to be for S.CA.C. members.

Robert telephoned the club secretary Bill Wilton to ask him if it would be okay for this one off occasion to have anglers from other clubs come to fish on Spigworth.

To Robert's surprise, Bill Wilton whole-heartedly endorsed the idea; Laurie and Bill were old friends.

Very shortly, Robert had 42 applicants wanting to participate, but this in itself proved to be a problem as there were only 37 swims to fish on Spigworth Pond. Robert sorted this problem out, there were only 36 out of the 37 available swims as Greenie's remains still occupied peg 9, 6 of those swims were quite large and could accommodate 2 men. Therefore, if there were 30 of the available swims pegged as one-man swims, the remaining six swims would be shared swims. The shared swim tickets would have an A & B added to them. When the anglers drew their tickets from the draw bag, the one's that drew swim 3A & 3B and so on were to fish in pairs in the same swim.

A strict dead bait only rule applied for this match, with only sea fish permissible. For those who don't know what a dead bait is, a pike's diet generally consists of fish and most of them would be alive, and some pike anglers use live fish for bait. Live baiting is, and has been for some time, a controversial subject. Some anglers feel that it is okay to use a live fish for bait as pike eat live fish anyway, whilst other anglers prefer not to on an ethical basis. Some anglers think it is just plain cruel.

Among the participants for this pike match was Walter Wigmore, keen as mustard to try for another species to catch; he hoped that this species would be less elusive than any other he had tried to catch. With fish used as bait for the pike match, at least Walter would be reeling in a fish every time whether he caught anything or not, even if it was a sprat from Mac Fisheries.

Two young anglers in their late teens responding to Robert Wansford's advert in the angling press were Jim Phillips and Dick Sperling from a small village in the Vernbury Vale called Vernham. Both were keen match anglers, Jim a greengrocer by trade was the better angler and regularly thrashed the pants off apprentice butcher Dick. Jim used to beat Dick in fishing matches also! For both Jim and Dick, this would be an adventure because neither of them had travelled outside the Vernbury Vale before.

The Shepherd and Crook proprietor Charlie Chatswell had been phoning various funeral directors, nearly falling over backwards when the first quote he received was £250, nearly 10 times as much as he was earning per week. But Charlie searched further and managed to get a more reasonable quote from William Dirge the Funeral Directors established 1879; £210 and a complimentary wreath thrown in.

Robert Wansford telephoned various fishing tackle shops, cheekily asking if they would donate items of tackle as prizes for this important pike match. The overwhelming enthusiasm from a number of tackle shop proprietors to contribute was completely unexpected. One tackle shop donated a 12ft 3½lb test curve pike rod built by local rod builder Midge Timpson. Some tackle shops weren't quite as generous, packets of treble hooks and maggot boxes being a typical example of their donations. One gift donated by a tackle shop was a hand warmer box with little charcoal sticks. When ignited, the charcoal sticks would smoulder inside the box for 5 hours or more, this would be a welcomed prize for the lucky angler that winter once the temperatures plummeted.

Charlie Chatswell telephoned Spinfield Hospital to find out how Dorothy Bluet was, there was good news. Dorothy would be able to go home at the weekend as long as somebody was prepared to care for her as she was still very poorly, even though she was off the critical list. Charlie's pub used to be an inn during the 19th Century, boasting five reasonably large rooms for lodgers and travellers that may have needed an overnight stop after a tiring journey. Charlie would prepare a room for Dorothy to stay in while she convalesced, hopefully she would be well enough for Laurie's funeral.

A few days later, with Dorothy discharged from Spinfield Hospital; Charlie Chatswell collected her and took her back to the pub to settle her in the room he had cleared out. He made sure the bed linen was clean and aired, and gave the room a scrupulous vacuum cleaning and dusting, fit for a princess.

During the drive back from the hospital, Dorothy expressed a slight worry that she may have left a saucepan of steak and kidney stewing on the gas stove when she took ill. To settle Dorothy's mind, Charlie told her not to worry because he was sure the ambulance men would have made sure to turn off anything they thought to be dangerous, but just to ease her mind, he promised to take her home to see that everything was okay.

On arrival to Dorothy's home, a nasty odour pervaded Charlie and Dorothy's nostrils as they walked in through the front doorway. Dorothy had indeed left a saucepan of steak and kidney on the stove, but the meat was still raw and Dorothy didn't even get around to adding any stock or liquid to the pan. A buzzing noise in the kitchen announced the fact that some houseflies had been having 'a bit of a knees up' in Dorothy's absence.

Cupping his hand over his mouth whilst retching, Charlie took the saucepan of rotten offal exploding with enthusiastic flies to the outside W.C. to flush it down the lavatory, and clean the saucepan out with the flush water at the same time. A few days later, the meat would have been wriggling with white maggots.

Dreadfully embarrassed by all of this, Dorothy offered to make a cup of tea for Charlie. The Bluets didn't own a refrigerator, just a marble slab to keep dairy products cool. Charlie said he'd check the milk to see if it was still fresh. As he sniffed the bottle, it became immediately evident that the milk was quite past its best. Again, with cupped hand over mouth and synchronised retching, Charlie poured the rancid milk down the kitchen sink, followed by a good helping of bleach and fresh water.

Charlie told Dorothy that it would be a good idea to switch off the electricity and gas supply while she was recuperating at the pub.

After ensuring that Dorothy had plenty of clean clothes to take with her, and checking that the backdoor was locked, Charlie pulled the front door shut and drove her to the pub.

Richard Wansford in the meantime had been busy trying to get friends and relations to sponsor him, so far, he had raised £5.25p. With luck, the other anglers participating in this special pike match would fair as well, if not better.

Back at home, Walter Wigmore was eagerly swotting up on pike fishing info from various books and magazines. He wanted so much to make an impact in this special match. Top tips from expert pike anglers seemed alien to him. Walter knew that it was important not to strike the pike on the first indication of a bite. However, little wrinkles of seemingly helpful advice in some of the old books such as 'When a pike takes your bait, smoke a packet of 5 Woodbine plain cigarettes and pop into your local pub for a pint of I.P.A. before striking' seemed a bit long winded. Surely, by the time you'd come back from the pub, the pike would have stripped most of your line from your reel, digested the fish bait and passed it out before you'd picked your rod up? Even an inexperienced pike angler like Walter could see this could cause problems and undoubtedly be detrimental to the well-being of such a magnificent creature. Walter decided that one cigarette would be enough, even if he didn't like Woodbine cigarettes, plain or filter tipped very much. Notwithstanding, Walter didn't relish the idea of popping into the pub for a pint of I.P.A. either, as he wasn't really much of a drinker apart from the odd port and lemon at Christmas. He was also uncertain of the safety in drinking Isopropyl Alcohol; a bottle of Schweppes Old English Ginger Ale would suffice.

Having finally settled Dorothy Bluet into her temporary home at The Shepherd and Crook, Charlie Chatswell prepared a meal for her. Her diet was something to consider as Dorothy had had a heart scare. The hospital gave her a list of the things she could eat, but somehow the things that she should avoid eating were missing from the list. Charlie telephoned Spinfield Hospital for advice, certainly Weetabix, boiled eggs, white fish, chicken and vegetables would become a bit limiting. Apparently, Dorothy had left a second page behind with advice on more things that she could eat and finally the list of foods to avoid. However, no worry, the hospital told Charlie what was on the do and don't list and he made note of them.

Charlie braved broaching the subject about Laurie Bluet's funeral to Dorothy, and told her it would be at 11:00am Thursday 9th October at Bunnington Cemetery. She was pleased that Charlie had been kind enough to arrange things for her while she was in hospital. The choice of coffin would be hers of course, and Charlie had obtained a brochure from the funeral director for her to peruse.

"William Dirge the Funeral Directors, established 1879! Is William still alive then?" questioned Dorothy.

"Well yes, but not the same William Dirge from 1879, the William that is there now is his grandson." Charlie said with a smile.

Charlie asked Dorothy if she would like any particular music played in the cemetery chapel. Dorothy thought it would be nice to play one of Laurie's favourite pieces of music, Moonlight Fiesta by Winifred Atwell.

"It's in his gramophone record collection in the lounge." said Dorothy.

"Is the tune on an LP?" asked Charlie.

"No, it's an old 78 that he's had since he was a young man. Oh, and he wouldn't like it played on one of those new fangled electrical record players. It will have to be played on his gramophone if they haven't got one in the chapel!" insisted Dorothy.

A neighbour had given Laurie a record player, but he just did not like the sound of it in comparison to his wind up gramophone, it sounded, well...too real!

Dorothy also insisted that Laurie should have his beloved greenheart fishing rod and wooden Nottingham reel with him in the casket; it is what Laurie would have wanted.

The arrangement for the pike match was in memoriam, Sunday 12th October. 8:00am sharp for the ticket draw, 8:30am start and the match finishing at 4:00pm.

Food and refreshments would be available with the kind help of ice cream mogul Paolo Mancini. Obviously, ice cream was unlikely to be very popular considering the time of year, but Paolo had also been successful with a fish & chip shop as an offshoot from his ice cream parlour, so he borrowed a hot food van for the occasion. Of course, for those who didn't like eating fish for whatever reason, there would also be burgers, saveloys, sausages and pies, all proceeds would go towards the funeral expenses.

With everyone imbibing hot tea and coffee on a cold day, the call of nature would happen at some juncture, so Robert Wansford arranged the installation of a Portaloo. This addition to personal comforts would be necessary if ladies were present, for the gentlemen, the nearest bush would be ideal.

On the 9th of October, the morning of Laurie Bluet's funeral, an eerie fog hung heavily over the village of Spigworth like a cold damp veil, like a shroud for all who mourned Antique Bluey.

At 10:30am, the funeral hearse appeared at the pub forecourt quietly with respect through the floating precipitation to a nervously waiting Dorothy. The second funeral car followed and Charlie placed his arm warmly around Dorothy's shoulders, guiding her little shaking body toward the rear seat as the driver opened the door.

The birds were silent that morning, apart from the usual irreverent squawk of a crow; the fog even subdued the usually busy and twittering sparrows in the privet hedges that lined the pub grounds.

The drive through the fog following Laurie's hearse to the chapel at Bunnington Cemetery, seemed like the longest journey of her life to Dorothy. Charlie sat in the back of the funeral car holding Dorothy's hand without a word, there was nothing to say in the circumstances.

Thoughts of her life with Laurie were milling around Dorothy's head, when they first met one evening at a dance in Holting Village Hall during his leave from Tanwell Airfield, how handsome and smart he looked in his air force uniform. She recalled their wedding day in November 1944, and how Laurie tripped and broke his nose at the altar, even then, she knew that Laurie was a buffoon but still she loved him.

Every Sunday morning, Laurie used to bring a cup of tea with a boiled egg and toast to her bed, the most horrid tasting cup of tea one could drink perhaps, but it was a loving cup!

In the summer, Laurie always made sure that there would be fresh flowers in a vase for Dorothy, even if mostly stolen from a neighbour's garden.

Dorothy thought of all the times she accused Laurie of being a lazy toad, he was lazy, but he was never too lazy to be romantic, some women don't even get that from their husbands!

The hearse and funeral car arrived at Bunnington Cemetery, driving through the archway at the entrance and toward the chapel. Headstones appeared like ghostly passing strangers in the billowing vapour.

At last, the cars stopped outside the chapel, Charlie looked up at the gargoyles under the roof of the chapel, gently dripping with water captured from the dense fog. The grotesque granite faces designed to ward off forces of evil as well as funnelling rainwater away from the sides of buildings appeared to serve only to ward off good to Charlie. The gargoyles were a haunting from his childhood and of his grandfather's funeral.

To Dorothy's surprise, she saw a large gathering of Laurie's mourners waiting outside the chapel, she had no idea that Laurie was so popular; to her he was just Laurie!

Four young pallbearers carried Laurie's coffin into the tiny chapel, a room steeped in centuries of sorrow. Laurie's wind-up gramophone was waiting on a table by his coffin during the ceremony.

"I hope you've put a new needle in Laurie's gramophone." said Dorothy, pointing at the ancient item of recorded music history.

"Oh, I don't think I did Dorothy." replied Charlie.

The Bluet's home was always damp, and Charlie had to cope with many silverfish crawling from the gramophone as he opened its lid, changing the needle was not a priority for him at the time.

"There's a little pull out draw on the front corner of the gramophone with a tiny yellow tin of needles inside, it says 'half tone' on the lid, Laurie didn't like his music too loud." said Dorothy.

Charlie pulled out the little lid and recoiled as three silverfish crawled over his hand. Brushing the horrid creatures from his hand in horror, Charlie braved opening the tin of needles. Charlie observed the beautiful design of the tin, with the His Master's Voice little dog Nipper's head cocked in wonderment, or confusion, listening to his master Francis Barraud's voice emanating from the cylinder phonograph's trumpet. To Charlie's relief, the little tin of needles read 'Half Tone' on the box.

"Make sure the gramophone is wound up properly, but don't over wind it or you'll brake the spring!" ordered Dorothy loudly, already sitting in her pew of choice.

Completely shaken by having orders barked at him in the chapel, Charlie found the crank handle for winding the gramophone up. Gently screwing the crank handle into the gramophone until it met resistance, Charlie proceeded to wind up the gramophone.

"SPOING!" said the gramophone as its spring snapped, being already wound up to its full tension.

Charlie continued turning the now limp crank handle to give the impression that he was still winding the gramophone up, and hoping that Dorothy hadn't noticed.

Dorothy hadn't noticed, she was deep in conversation with one of her neighbours Edie Trussett, who had popped in for a bit of a weep, and hopefully a cup of tea and a slice of Victoria Sponge after the ceremony.

As the throng of friends who came to pay their respect to Laurie Bluet slowly made their way to their seats in the chapel, Charlie had a quick and quiet word about his gramophone predicament to the Reverend Ronald Stirrup. Ronald Stirrup would soon lead the ceremony with a short sermon and a couple of hymns chosen by Dorothy.

"No problem." said Reverend Ronald Stirrup calmly, adding that there was a record player in the vestry that played records at all speeds, including the correct ones, 16, 33⅓, 45 & 78 rpm. He would record the 78-rpm disc onto a cassette recorder using a 5-pin DIN cord; and then play the recording over the speakers in the chapel. With a reduction of bass frequency, Dorothy would be none the wiser.

"Are you certain that Dorothy won't notice?" asked Charlie desperately.

"No, she won't notice, by the time I've finished my wonderfully solemn sermon, Dorothy will be filled with so much grief that she won't aware of anything."

Reverend Ronald Stirrup assured Charlie with assertion and a cocky wink.

To add a touch of realism, Reverend Ronald Stirrup switched a varispeed knob on the turntable of the record player to gently slow down the record whilst recording onto cassette, to sound as though the gramophone hadn't been wound up enough, this DJ like technique and performance would be replayed from the cassette player – genius!

The funeral service was kindly, very short, and sweet.

"Anyone who knew Laurie Bluet well will know that he loved listening to music, and one of his favourite musicians was Winifred Atwell. We will now listen to one of Laurie's favourite pieces of music before Laurie is taken to his place of rest." said Reverend Ronald Stirrup as an epilogue to his sermon.

The Reverend nodded to Charlie as a signal to play the record as he quickly went back to the vestry to press the play button of the cassette player.

Charlie mimed through the motions as though to put the tone arm onto the record to play it.

Unfortunately, Reverend Ronald wasn't told which side to record. Intuitively but wrongly, he recorded the A side The Story of Three Loves, Moonlight Fiesta was the B side, or flipside as all the hip disc jockeys loved to say.

Charlie looked at Dorothy in horror. Dorothy smiled and mouthed the words 'thank you' to him.

Charlie was astonished that Dorothy didn't appear to notice that the wrong tune was being played. Truth to tell, Dorothy wouldn't have been able to discern Moonlight Fiesta from Get Off My Cloud by The Rolling Stones, she didn't really take any notice of

Laurie's records, she only knew that was his favourite tune because he told her it was.

By the time the ceremony had finished, the Sun had burned off the fog to reveal a lovely sunny mild day. Once Laurie's coffin had been lowered into his grave and the first handful of soil was thrown by Dorothy, it was time for all to go to The Shepherd and Crook for a wake organised by Charlie Chatswell.

The wake was nothing too extravagant, sandwiches, sausage rolls and pork pies, and to Edie Trussett's relief and delight, a Victoria Sponge.

After the wake, Dorothy said to Charlie, "I think I'd like to go back home soon."

Charlie told Dorothy that he'd get Spigworth surgery's Doctor Ascot to visit the following day to see if she was fit enough to look after herself.

Edie Trussett told Charlie not to worry, as she would be looking after Dorothy when she returned home.

One thing Dorothy told Charlie that he didn't know about Laurie, was that he'd engraved his initials along with other airmen from his airbase on one of the oak pillars in the pub. Laurie, based at Tanwell Airfield, 18 miles West of Spigworth during the Second World War, used to fly Hawker Hurricanes. After the war, Tanwell became a military aviation museum.

"I'd like to visit Tanwell someday soon, as a tribute to Laurie, you know." said Dorothy.

Dorothy pointed to another engraving in the oak pillar; it said LB 4 DE 16.08.1940.

"Well look at that! Well I never, I'd forgotten that Laurie had done that, that's us, Laurie Bluet and Dorothy Ecclestone!" said Dorothy, adding that while they were there, Tanwell had been dive bombed by Stukas and a lot of men and planes were lost.

"I'm not sure if Laurie was supposed to be here with me or not that day, but I'm glad he was because he could have been killed as well." Dorothy mused.

7:30am Sunday morning, 12th of October 1975 saw 42 keen pike anglers waiting impatiently for the draw. The night had been a cold one, and only an hour of cloud cover during the early hours prevented a frost forming, and worse still, Spigworth Pond freezing over. The air was very cold and the anglers steaming breath made it difficult to differentiate the smokers from the non-smokers. The looks of embarrassment and annoyance on the smokers' faces, who'd been puffing on a long extinguished roll up, only to find that they'd been exhaling vapour from their breath were a sight to behold.

8:00am and Head Bailiff Mark Gosling took the bag of tickets around for the anglers to draw. The odd disappointed face when an angler drew a swim they didn't like was obviously to be expected, but not the sight of an angler bursting into tears like Peter Burt did when he drew a ticket for a shared swim that would see him paired with Walter Wigmore!

Walter was extremely offended by this melodramatic outburst from Squirt, he didn't enjoy the idea of being lumbered with the little creep either, but this day was supposed to be in memory of a very nice old man, and that level of selfish and childish reaction was totally unnecessary.

"You are a very loathsome and despicable little man, I'm not particularly keen on sharing a swim with you either, but I will endure it purely for respect of Laurie Bluet!" said Walter sternly.

"Ooh! Get you! Get out of the wrong side of bed this morning did we?" said Squirt with sarcasm.

Walter ignored Squirt's remark, picked up his fishing gear and walked to the swim he had drawn.

Mark Gosling grabbed hold of Squirt's collar as he walked past and said, "Anymore trouble from you Squirt and I will personally disqualify you from the pike match and ban you from fishing here for the remaining season. You got me?"

"Okay Mark, don't do that, I thought we were friends." whimpered Squirt.

"FRIENDS? Don't make me laugh!" Mark sneered.

Visiting anglers Jim Phillips and Dick Sperling from the remote village of Vernham, nestled deep in the Vernbury Vale, drove 132 miles to fish Laurie's memorial pike match. They were both delighted to have drawn shared swim tickets.

Jim Phillips had brought his favourite selection of pike baits, smoked peppered mackerel and Arbroath Smokies. Titter ye not thou great disbeliever, Jim had much success with these unusual baits!

Dick Sperling's choice of bait wasn't as exotic, herrings and sprats being his penchant.

Walter Wigmore had read that sardines can be very successful, but chose not to use them because they seemed a bit soft from a tin, and after a bit of experiment by squeezing them onto a treble hook he still wasn't convinced that they would be firm enough to stay on during a cast. Walter didn't realise that you could buy them fresh from the fishmongers. His local fishmongers was all out of oily round fish such as sprats, herring and mackerel, so Walter was palmed off with a few small dabs; if there was prize for bait originality in this pike match, he would win hands down. Luckily, for Walter, fishing tackle shop owner Ken Truman took heart and gave him some blast frozen sand eels and mackerel strips with his purchase of Alasticum trace wire and treble hooks. Wire traces are very important as a pike's teeth will sever the thickest of nylon lines, unless of course the nylon is about as thick as a tent's guy rope. Me thinks, a bit impossible to thread through and tie a knot in the treble hook perhaps!

Many of the anglers were not regular pike anglers and went to the great trouble of buying rods strong enough to catch and land a sizeable pike; such was their true respect for Laurie Bluet.

Although fishing with two rods was normally acceptable for pike fishing, Robert Wansford set the rule for one rod only in this match.

Spinning artificial lures was acceptable but with caution, making sure not to snag other anglers' lines in adjoining swims by such activity. With Walter Wigmore's casting prowess, it was sensible for him to abstain from spinning altogether.

After a false start, thanks to ever flatulent Graham 'Gruffer' Wheeldon letting a rather loud one go, fooling many anglers into casting in too early, the claxon horn bellowed its trumpety tone to start the match at 8:30am. Spigworth Pond's calm surface was disturbed by 42 loud splashes of dead sea fish belly flopping into the depths.

Settled into their shared swim, even if uncomfortably, Walter Wigmore and Squirt sat and waited in silence as though they were in swims of their own.

Walter tried to make conversation with Squirt, "It was quite chilly this morning wasn't it Peter?"

"Really? Can't say I've noticed!" replied Squirt without making eye contact with Walter

"Still, it feels a little milder now." said Walter to no reply.

Walter continued to break the ice with Squirt for the next five minutes; there was one brief glimpse of hope when he offered a Sharp's Extra Strong Mint to him.

Squirt snatched the mint from Walter's packet and mumbled "Cheers."

Shortly after, all human contact seemed to go cold for Walter and Squirt.

Fishing that particular day were the three camp carpers, Will Spring, Jed Cleminson and Rick Western. They had forsaken their usual sartorial elegance for something a little more manly for this special occasion, purely out of respect for Laurie. Their carp rods were strong enough to land any pike that lurked in the watery environment of Spigworth Pond, unlike some of the anglers that day who had bought pike rods especially for the occasion.

Jim Phillips and Dick Sperling from Vernham had settled in nicely and were enjoying the experience of fishing somewhere far from home. For some of the natives of their village, a trip outside of the Vernbury Vale was like going abroad; very few Vernhamites ever left the village, let alone the Vale!

Jim Phillips, a greengrocer by trade, normally competed in general coarse fishing matches and was very successful. His finest match win was with 3lbs of 3-spined sticklebacks in the summer league final of 1973 on Poddum Creek, a tributary stream of the River Poddum. One might find sticklebacks an odd choice as a target species for a fishing match. However, the sticklebacks in the Vernbury Vale grew large, 2 drams not being that uncommon. With 126 drams in a pound, that is still a lot of sticklebacks and only goes to show how hard Jim fished in his matches. He caught them using a very tiny maggot called 'Squiglets' supplied by his angling buddy Dick Sperling.

Dick, a butcher's apprentice used to scrounge the odd cut of meat that was past its best from his uncle and butcher's shop proprietor Frank Sperling. Offal such as livers, kidneys and hearts were often unsold, and Dick found these meaty treats were most attractive to a certain species of fly unique to the Vernbury Vale called 'The Poddum Fly'. This tiny fly never wandered from the Vernbury Vale, even if blown off course it would eventually find its way back, or die. The Poddum Fly larvae were extremely small and were ideal for catching tiddlers, sticklebacks and minnows loved them.

However, this would not help Dick or Jim in the pike match on Spigworth Pond, there they would have to use their watercraft skills to their maximum.

When general coarse anglers have a bash at pike fishing, their approach to tackle and bait presentation is always a bit interesting.

Badger Bill, the Fred J Taylor freak, could not resist using his beloved 'lift method' with a sprat as bait for this match, and indeed the presentation would give him the same excitement if a pike picked up his bait. There would be no doubt when a pike had the bait in its mouth as the float would pop up and lay flat on the surface of the pond.

Paolo Mancini arrived at around 9:00am in the borrowed hot food van, and by 10:30am, the aromas of fish and chips, hot dogs and burgers enticed every nostril present. Paolo had also brought a small supply of Bolognese for the more adventurous scoffer, but he had substituted the spaghetti with fusilli pasta. Spaghetti can be frustrating enough to wrestle with at the dinner table, but on the bank and a plate on your knee, one would probably give up and throw the whole lot into the pond!

At 11:12am, the first bit of predatory action came to, unbelievably, Walter Wigmore! After a 2-minute fight, Walter slipped a lovely 3lb 5oz perch over the mesh of his landing net. A magnificent fish and a pond record at that, unfortunately for Walter this was a pike match and so didn't count. Poor old Walter!

Jim Phillips from Vernham received some unwanted attention from a swan as it waddled up the bank to scrounge one of his Arbroath Smokies. Jim Phillips was an extreme ornithophobic, but not with a fear of birds in general, his phobia was particularly of swans. After a knee-pecking incident when he was wearing shorts as a schoolboy, he developed a fear of swans. Cygnophobia would be the name of his irrational fear, if the word existed. Poor old Jim ran for his life when that swan appeared, but Dick Sperling managed to make the bird go away by throwing a cheese sandwich far out from the bank into the pond. One of Jim's sandwiches of course, it was only fair!

At 12:43pm, Jed Cleminson's Heron bite indicator let out a shrill note as something had picked up his ledgered mackerel bait and tore away at a rate of knots, stripping line of the reel spool. Jed picked up the rod, closed the bale arm of his reel with a decisive clunk, and pulled the rod back with a gentle strike to set the hooks. Suddenly, Jed's angling world went completely mad as a cormorant surfaced from the depths and took off with the mackerel bait in its beak. It took a while for Jed to convince the cormorant that it wasn't a good idea to fly off with the tethered fish before it finally let go. That could have been nasty if the bird had the treble hooks in its mouth!

The first pike of the day came to the match organizer Robert Wansford, only a 3lb Jack Pike, but it still counted. Robert found the fishing very slow, it wasn't that the pike weren't actively hunting for food, but rather that they were distracted by the shoals of many small roach, the occasional explosion of tiddlers on the surface was testament to that. Why pick a dead herring when you can suck in an exciting gobfull of whitebait?

One sea fish that was proving very popular in this special pike match was Paolo Mancini's beautifully battered haddock with a huge bag of piping hot chips as an accompaniment on a bitterly cold day. Who cares about the fishing? Even villagers of Spigworth were following their noses to find themselves on the banks of Spigworth Pond to buy fish and chips.

Dorothy Bluet appeared and took a toddle round the pond to thank all the anglers for their participation. The bankside was very muddy and little sling-back patent leather shoes weren't the ideal choice of footwear that day, Dorothy's nylons got a bit grubby too!

Walter Wigmore was still eager to break the ice and soothe the discomfort of embarrassing silence with Squirt. The odd grunts of yes and no from Squirt were about all to expect, until Walter talked about his favourite book Mr Crabtree Goes Fishing. It transpired that this book was also Squirt's favourite bedtime reading as a child. With the bedside light on, a glass of milk and a plate of Malted Milk biscuits with a lump of Caerphilly cheese, this book would send little Peter Burt off to sleep to dream of shiny silver roach flashing in the summer sunlight.

Peter's childhood wasn't always happy, his Scottish dad Oswald Burt was a hardened drinker who was quite useful with his fists.

Many was the time when Oswald would get home early and very drunk, and young Peter didn't move quickly enough to "Get oot 'o ma way will ye, afore I belt ye, ye awfy wee mongrel!", ending up with a black eye, split lip, or both. Oswald never intended to hurt his beloved little boy, it was just because he was so often extremely depressed and he couldn't control his rage.

Coupled with being teased and bullied for dressing in dirty clothes and being a bit smelly at school, this personal torment had shaped little Peter Burt into the obnoxious piece of pooh that people had learned to despise.

Walter Wigmore realised somehow that Squirt deep down had a very nice fellow inside him just waiting to surface, and that there was something from way back in his childhood that made him the way he was. Walter intended to make the nice Squirt surface!

The weird pair from Vernham, Jim Phillips and Dick Sperling, like most of the other anglers, weren't having any luck with the pike at all, despite all the predator activity in front of them. There were at least two pike marauding and menacing the shoals of baby roach near the reeds either side of their swim. Jim Phillips tried casting past the commotion and reeling the bait back in slowly, allowing it to gently roll and wobble through the shoals of roach in an attempt to attract the attention of the needle toothed beast.

Dick sat and ate a banana as he watched Jim trying to lure the pike into grabbing his bait. After finishing the banana, Dick threw the banana skin making it land on top of Jim's head gently. The banana skin looked rather like one of those pointless hats that women wear on Ladies Day at Royal Ascot. Jim didn't flinch and carried on fishing.

"You may as well be using that banana skin as bait for all the luck your having with that smoked mackerel." chuckled Dick.

"What a brilliant idea Dick!" replied Jim excitedly.

Jim reeled in the smoked peppered mackerel, unhooked it and threw it at Dick as he opened his mouth to yawn. A perfect shot, the mackerel flew straight into Dick's wide-open mouth. Dick choked, spluttered and swore at Jim.

Jim impaled the banana skin on his treble hooks in a similar fashion to that of the smoked mackerel bait. Flicking the banana skin out beyond the shoal of baby roach, Jim gently turned his reel handle to allow the strange yellow offering to gently wobble and flap in the water.

There was a huge swirl in the water as a pike made a lunge for the banana skin and suddenly Jim was doing battle with the biggest pike he had ever seen in his life. The fight was short lived but spectacular, within three minutes Jim was drawing the pike towards his landing net. As the pike finally submitted, it came gently with its eyes just above the surface like a crocodile.

With Jim's pike landed, Mark Gosling arrived with the official Spinfield Coarse Angling Club weighing scales. The needle on the dial scale stopped on 17lb 4oz. It was going to be very hard for any of the other anglers in this special pike match to compete with that!

At 3 o'clock precisely, Badger Bill's float popped up and laid on the surface of the pond before slowly slipping away. Bill gently swept his rod back to set the hooks into the jaws of the predator. As the line tightened, Bill felt a solid resistance on the other end. Within moments though, he recognised the sickening tumbling sensation through his rod as that of a very large eel. Still, it was a bit of unexpected action for the time of year on an otherwise blank day for Bill.

The eel incidentally weighed 4lbs exactly if anyone is interested!

From 3 o'clock until a quarter to 4, the time lumbered slowly like a brontosaurus with a broken back leg.

Walter Wigmore told squirt that he was going to reel in and pack up, as he had no confidence in catching anything before the final blast of the claxon.

As he reeled in, Walter felt a sudden thump on the end of his line. Alarmingly, something of mammoth proportion was pulling violently and stripping line from Walter's reel spool at a frightening rate. The fish, a pike in the 25lb region came to the surface and tail-walked like a blue marlin on the Pacific Ocean. As many an experienced pike angler knows, it can be a time for a pike to shed the hooks whilst tail-walking. Not for Walter, this fish stayed on and fought like a dog.

"I don't mind telling you Peter, I am a little bit frightened of this fish." said Jim worriedly.

"You shouldn't be Walter, you seem to be doing all the right things with it." said Squirt assuredly.

Walter found a new gained confidence in himself with Squirt's encouraging words and was able to play the fish admirably.

As the pike began to tire, Walter asked Squirt if he could assist him in landing the fish. Squirt was touched that anyone could ask him for help, but now he was nervous in case he loused up the landing of Walter's pike.

As Walter drew the gargantuan pike toward the landing net which was wielded by Squirt, he noticed that only one of the treble hooks was delicately nicked in a thin fold of skin at the edge of its mouth.

"We'll have to be careful here Peter, the hook is only just holding!" Walter warned Squirt.

Both anglers had been completely unaware that they had drawn an audience of excited anglers to witness the landing of a possible Spigworth Pond record pike.

Abruptly and typically rudely, Gruffer Wheeldon broke the silence with one of his mallard duck imitating trouser trumpets.

This unexpected noise made Squirt jump and he stumbled as the pike neared the front of Walter's landing net, knocking it off the light hook hold. They watched the leviathan slowly turn away, to disappear into the dark depths.

The audience of spectators behind sighed and gasped with shock, and then a stunned silence.

Squirt looked at Walter and burst into tears.

"Why are you so upset Peter?" asked Walter with a kindly tone.

"I've ruined your special moment with a fish that could have made you the hero of Antique Bluey's pike match!" sobbed Squirt.

"Do you know Peter, from the moment I hooked that fish, I knew it wasn't going to be mine." said Walter.

"Well it's very kind of you to be so forgiving, others may not have been so chivalrous." whimpered Squirt.

"At least we got to see the fish Peter, which is almost as good as landing it!" Walter conceded as he smiled.

A huge round of applause erupted from the spectators and match organiser Robert Wansford congratulated Walter for playing the pike so expertly.

At 4:00pm, the claxon let out its raucous blast to end the match. First prize went to Jim Phillips of Vernham for the biggest pike of the match, second prize went to Robert Wansford for the little Jack pike, and third prize went to Walter Wigmore for showing such grace in defeat.

Antique Bluey's pike match managed to raise £297.73 ½ p in sponsorship, three and a half pence being donated by 7 year old Daisy Watkins from Spigworth village. The three and a half pence was the change from the chips Daisy bought from Paolo Mancini incidentally, and was the last of her pocket money…Ah! Bless!

With the funeral and the wake paid for by the sponsorship money, the balance of the sponsorship went to Dorothy. Charlie Chatswell encouraged Dorothy to buy a fridge / freezer and dispense with the marble slab.

"Oh no, the marble slab must stay, Laurie liked his butter to be kept on the marble slab!" insisted Dorothy.

CHAPTER 7

NOVEMBER TENCH

November is unlike October where the ghosts of the summer countryside remind us that they were once there, the lily pads still green and buoyant and reed mace only just showing signs of decay. November pronounces the death of bank side foliage and shelter for wildlife, the sad lily pads brown and rot, and for some faint-hearted anglers, it's the end of their personal coarse fishing season. The changing of the clocks from BST to GMT on the last Sunday of October only adds to the misery.

The lion-hearted angler will fish on in implacable earnest, believing that while there is water, there will be fish to catch! In addition, when that water is frozen, attempts to break the ice will be made to create a suitable fishing hole. If that ice becomes too thick with the progressive cold snaps that can occur in the Northern Hemisphere, it is time to stay at home, clean and tidy up the fishing tackle in preparation for a thaw.

What madness is it that draws a seemingly intelligent and sane person from their warm bed on a cold Winter Saturday morning? What lunacy is it that makes a person sit by a pond or river with an icy Siberian blast stiffening their faces?
    Only the children that once stared through a jarful of sticklebacks or minnows and saw their destiny can answer those questions.

7:30am, Saturday November 7th 1975, found Badger Bill Parsons scrunching through some light frost with hopes of catching a late season tench.

"Hello Badger, what are fishing for today?" said Mark Gosling as he impaled a rather large lobworm on a number 6 hook.

"Ah, the same fish that I always fish for." said Badger with a smile.

"Are you mad?" questioned a startled Mark Gosling.

"Possibly Mark, we'll see." replied Badger with a giggle.

"You can't catch a tench after September!" all the experts said, Badger thought otherwise. Once the temperature of Spigworth Pond dropped during autumn, the water became crystal-clear, clear enough to see almost every detail of the pond bed. Badger had spent a number of winters observing fish movement by climbing trees, wearing polarised sunglasses to remove as much surface glare as possible.

From the vantage point of a tree, Badger saw dark shapes, too small to be carp, slowly moving and possibly feeding. There was absolutely no doubt in Badger's mind that tench were active, even through winter!

Badger's approach to catching tench in the winter was completely different to his summer technique of lift method float fishing, Badger would be ledgering.

During previous winters, Badger had noticed some odd very slow bites on his swing-tip indicator screwed into the end of his legering rod. The bites were hardly noticeable, they were more of a gentle tightening of the line and then slackening off as soon as the fish felt any resistance.

It seemed to Badger, that although fish are cold blooded and slow down a bit when the water temperature drops to preserve valuable energy, their senses may be reasonably sharp, indeed maybe their caution is still as sharp.

Badger's winter ledger rig had typically been a hook length of 18 inches from ledger weight to hook; maybe it was the confidence of distance travelled after picking bait up that a tench needed to commit itself to accepting the found morsel of food as safe.

For any fish that has been caught before, there has to be a safe distance limit to travel without resistance when sampling alien food samples such as maggots, bread or whatever before deeming the food as safe. Once that fish commits itself to that particular item of nutrition, it reaches a point of no return.

Badger reasoned that it could be a distance of 3 feet before his quarry felt safe to scoff the bait, so he tied a 3 feet 6 inch length hook length to offer his bait.

Now for the prefect bait, Badger's experience with maggots proved tiresome with scores of small roach picking up his bait, great on a cold winter's day for the average angler, but not for Badger. He needed a different type of bait for old tinca tinca, and with the water so cold, a stinky one!

Knowing that tench had a penchant for savoury baits in his experience, he had read of carp anglers having reasonable success in the winter using tinned cat food blended into a paste by kneading it with plain flour.

Badger found the experience of pressing Jellymeat Whiskers into a paste quite nauseating to say the least, but if the pukeworthy concoction proved successful, he could grow to get used to it, even if not like it.

For just over a week, Badger had been visiting his chosen swim every morning before work to introduce a small amount of the cat food paste, this day would hopefully show whether the bait would be acceptable to the fish or not!

Ever-keen angler Walter Wigmore and Peter 'Squirt' Burt were there also that cold November morning. Walter brought Squirt in his car, it appeared that a sort of friendship cemented between Walter and Squirt since the Antique Bluey memorial pike competition. Squirt had also written his own car off recently after driving into a ditch, so that did seem to blur the reality of companionship a bit.

The fantasy friendship that Squirt had with Head Bailiff Mark Gosling was now over, but Mark felt pleased that Squirt had found someone to fish with, even if it was because he didn't have to put up with Squirt following him about all over the place anymore.

"Now you don't have to share a swim with me just because I gave you a lift here Peter, you may fish wherever you wish." said Walter with a kindly smile.

"What sort of soup have you got in your flask then Walter?" said Squirt with an abstract answer.

"Um, cream of tomato Peter, why?" questioned Walter.

"Have you got any bread with it?" asked Squirt with a slightly more relevance.

"I've made some mature cheddar cheese and pickle sandwiches." said a confused Walter.

"I'll swap you a scotch egg for a cup of soup and a sandwich then, and it would make sense for us to share the same swim with all this food swapping going on." said Squirt.

Walter laughed heartedly, this was the happiest he had felt for many years. Walter was also aware that this happiness might not last long once Squirt had his transport situation sorted out, so he resigned himself to enjoy the ephemeral friendship while he could.

In the near distance, one could hear the noise of excited children and adults adding the final touches to the bonfire, in preparation for the Spigworth village bonfire party.

At 6:00pm on the first Saturday in November, Spigworth closed the village to outsiders, the Spigworth bonfire party was exclusive.

A light wind stirred, and the crackling fragrance of fried bacon drifted across the pond, received by the hungry nostrils of Badger Bill Parsons. The camp carp anglers three, Will Spring, Jed Cleminson and Rick Western had awoken for morning breakfast.

Will, Jed and Rick had been there overnight without a single bleep on their buzzers, although it has to be said that none of them would have heard their buzzers at all after the skin-full of beer they'd consumed in The Shepherd and Crook on the previous evening. Rick became very aware at one point in the night that his army surplus bivouac had collapsed on him. He was too sozzled to think about getting out from his sleeping bag to put the situation right, he just accepted that he had a rather large blanket wrapped around him, and that could only insulate him even more from the cold.

Jed had vague memories of getting out of his bivouac for tiddle during the night and toppling into the reeds as he tried to stand straight on an uneven bank; this situation most likely aided and abetted by six pints of local brew he had scooped back in the pub the night before.

Will didn't remember anything!

Badger did his best to ignore the smell of smoky porcine rashers and poured out a cup of coffee from his thermos flask to take his mind off the sizzling torment, it didn't work! Badger had only eaten a slice of toast and marmalade that morning, his stomach was growling like a bear.

"Hey Baldy, fancy a bacon sarnie love?" Rick shouted across the pond to Badger.

"Er, no thanks Rick, I don't want to leave my rod unattended." replied Badger with a loud wheezing whisper, so as not to disturb the fish.

"It's alright poppet, I'll bring it round for you if you like?" offered Rick.

"No, no, I'm alright thank you!" said Badger, hoping that would be the last he would hear about the subject of bacon sandwiches proffered by a carp angler in drag with smeared mascara and morning stubble.

"Suit yourself then lovey, you can't say I didn't offer!" hissed Rick.

The top of Badger's head was getting cold, so he pulled a woolly pom-pom hat on to keep it warm. Annoyingly for Badger, he'd forgotten to shave his Fred J Taylor bald pate that morning, and the woollen hat snagged on the rough re-growth of hair. It isn't easy trying to maintain the Fred J look if you aren't really bald. Crikey, even Yul Brynner and Telly Savalas worked hard to keep their manes repressed, and yet, they themselves may have been already bald without knowing!

A loud ripping noise like the ripping of strong canvas reverberated in the Spigworth air; everyone knew that it was Graham 'Gruffer' Wheeldon announcing his presence. Graham had only put his bait in for a quarter of an hour and he was already winching in some reasonable roach, his maggots anointed with vanilla essence were doing their business.

Gruffer never once used a rod rest for anything other than resting his rod when baiting up or changing tackle, he held his hollow fibre glass rod all the time and very rarely did he miss a bite. Nonetheless, as light as his rod was in comparison to the old solid glass rods, he did start to suffer with repetitive strain injury through the constant holding and casting with his beloved float rod. The dream of the carbon fibre and graphite rod was still to be realised, these were materials that only aerospace technology was privileged to enjoy.

Walter Wigmore and Squirt hadn't caught a single fish. Squirt actually missed a few bites, but he wouldn't have known because he was too busy talking about Mr Crabtree with Walter.

"Of course Peter, I've struggled to influence my children in the ways of Mr Crabtree, but they just don't want to know." said a pensive Walter.

"At least you've been able to take your kids fishing, I haven't with mine." said Squirt sadly.

"I had no idea you had children Peter, do they live with you?" asked Walter.

Squirt explained to Walter how he was once married and had a little son and daughter, but by some twist of unfair fate, his wife left him for a friend of his Scottish cousin from his father's side. His cousin Dougie had come down with his best friend Alex from Inverness to visit him for a short while. In that short while, his wife Sally fell in love with Alex and took off with him.

"Oh that's terrible Peter, did you ever see them again?" asked Walter.

"I drove all the way to Inverness a few years ago with the idea of staying for a few days when Sally said I could see the kids. Unfortunately when I got there, Sally had made other plans so I was only able to see them for a short while, the sad bit is that they didn't even know who I was and were very wary of me, like a stranger." said Squirt with sorrow.

Squirt shook himself to extinguish his melancholy mood and said, "Anyway, what's this got to do with fishing? Let's get some kippers in the net!"

"Quite right Peter, quite right!" Walter concurred.

Badger, had started getting a few tentative bites on his cat food paste baits, it appeared that something liked the taste of old Jelly Meat Whiskers.

Suddenly, Badger had an extremely violent bite on his swing tip, his reel was churning as a very determined fish charged off for freedom having realised its mistake. As soon as Badger picked his rod up and swept it back into a strike, he knew it was a carp, disappointment consumed his joy.

After 10 minutes of playing the fish that had ruined Badger's bait presentation, a 15lb leather carp slipped over his ungrateful landing net. Shouts and jeers of 'jammy bald git!' and 'fluke!' from the camp carp anglers three, only irritated him more.

However, it didn't take long for Jed 'hello sweetie!' Cleminson to mince his way around to Badger's side of the pond to ask Badger what he was using for bait.

"Ooh! That's a nice kipper Bill! What are you using for bait lovey?" enquired Jed with a shrill note of excitement to his voice.

Not wishing to give his secret away, Badger grunted "Mother's Pride!"

"What, bread?" gasped Jed.

"Yep, good old ready sliced white bread." Badger lied.

"Phew! What's that fishy smell?" Jed grimaced.

"Oh, that'll be my pilchard sandwiches." replied Badger with a fib of Pinocchio nose proportion.

Still very hung-over, Jed ran for the nearest bush and wretched with heaving shoulders. After the violent vomiting, Jed returned to Will and Rick with no other info than 'it was pure luck with bread as bait!'

Badger returned the leather carp, unhooked, unharmed and un-weighed to its cold liquid abode. Jed, Will and Rick would go home later on that Saturday evening without a single bite to their specialist carp tackle and baits, scratching their heads as to why an angler could be so annoyed to catch one of their favourite species and not even bother to weigh it. Perhaps they would have been equally annoyed if a tench picked up one of their baits intended for carp.

Nevertheless, with all of this specialist pretentiousness, as far as many anglers in 1975 were concerned, carp and tench would sleep in the bottom mud all winter and weren't worth the effort.

Walter Wigmore and Squirt had caught a few small roach each to keep them interested on that cold November day, both of them enjoying each other's company, and food.

At 2:00pm, Graham 'Gruffer' Wheeldon's stomach was feeling uncomfortable, and so he decided to pack his gear away and leave, in particular after thinking he was going to break wind and discovering that he was quite wrong! That was possibly the most difficult drive home for poor old Graham.

Mark Gosling reeled in to get up out of his chair and stretch his legs for a while. On his walk, Mark decided to have a chat with Badger and see how he was getting on with the tench.
"Hello Badger, had anything yet?" enquired Mark.
"Nothing from the tench, no, I did have a carp a while ago though." replied Badger.
"A carp?" said a startled Mark.
"Yeah, a leather about 15lbs." said Badger.
"I bet you're chuffed then Badger?" said Mark.
"No, not really, I'd have preferred it to be a tench." said Badger.
Mark Gosling walked away saying that he still thought Badger was mad, and that if anybody caught a tench that day, he would eat one of his own worms.
"I'll hold you to that Mark!" said Badger.
Mark Gosling returned to his swim, impaled a fresh lobworm on his hook and flicked it 15 feet out in front of him.
As his bait hit the water, Mark observed a small cluster of tiny bubbles nearby on the surface. Even though the bubbles looked as though a tench had made them, Mark maintained his belief that you couldn't catch tench during the winter.
10 minutes had passed since casting out, and Mark poured himself a cup of coffee from his thermos flask. As Mark put the cup to his lip for a sip of piping hot

beverage, his fishing rod started jumping up and down in its rod rests and his fishing reel spinning backwards as line stripped from it as a very alarmed fish ran off for freedom.

As most anglers would react in this situation, Mark spilled the steaming coffee all over his legs. Many anglers have found themselves in this predicament, sitting biteless for hours and deciding to have a hot drink to relieve the boredom seems to summon up a bite from nowhere. This predicament can also occur when bursting to go for a wee wee but desperately holding on in case one misses a bite. Eventually when the call of nature becomes a primal scream and one just can't hold on anymore, one either misses a bite or returns to the swim to find their fishing reels churning in a frenzy. This is of course is the reason why electronic bite indicators were invented, to put the fear of Hades into you when you are in mid-stream urination, this effect can be even more poignant during the hours of pitch-black darkness!

Grasping for his rod and reel, Mark struck into the fish, feeling a solid angry resistance.

"Are you in Mark?" shouted Badger.

"Yep, I think it's a carp!" replied Mark excitedly.

Badger reeled in to visit Mark's swim and watch the action.

"It's fighting hard isn't it Mark?" said Badger.

"Yep, I reckon it's a carp!" replied.

"Are you sure it's not a tench?" asked Badger, certain that Mark had hooked a tench.

"No, you can't catch tench in the winter unless you foul hook them." claimed Mark with dogged certainty.

As Mark played the fish and it began to tire, Badger told him that he was 100% certain that a tench was about to be gracing the landing net.

Mark replied in agitation "You just won't give up will you? As I told you before this isn't a tench, it's a…TENCH!"

"Yep, that's right Mark! How do you want your worms, on their own or between two slices of bread?" laughed Mark.

As Mark drew the tench over his landing net, tears welled up in his eyes. In all his pig-headed, cock-sure life, Mark had never been so pleased to be so wrong.

Badger noticed that the hook length Mark was only about 2 feet long. Maybe his theory regarding length of hook length was wrong. Mark preferred to keep the hook length at that distance between hook and weight because he felt it gave him better bite registration, it also prevented perch from gorging the worm down deep into their throats, as he would see the bite before they had the chance to swallow.

Mark weighed the tench in a large polythene carrier bag with the weighing scales hook in its handles, the scale's needle settled on 3lb 2oz.

"Well done Mark" said Badger in a congratulatory tone.

Badger took a photo of Mark and the tench with Mark's camera.

Leaving Mark to return to his swim, Badger remarked with a smirk "Well, I suppose I ought to go back and try to catch one myself. that is of course if you can catch tench in the winter?"

"Shaddup baldy!" was Mark's response.

Badger returned to his swim and within a half of an hour of casting out he himself was into a tench, but this one was bigger than Mark's fish.

After 5 minutes, Badger had battled with and landed a tench of 5lbs 1oz, his pungent bait seemed to be working.

By 4:30pm, Badger had caught another tench, this time a little smaller weighing 4lb 4oz.

In the 21st Century, when reading about the weights of Badger's tench, one may think that fish of that size as run of the mill. In 1975 however, with the British record being a little over 8lbs, those tench were true specimens!

With the daylight fading fast and windless air, small roach dimpled the flat calm surface of Spigworth Pond.

The racket of satisfied anglers rattling their stainless steel bank sticks and packing up their tackle competed with the quacking of a very angry and excited mallard ducks reverberating around the pond. The anglers' already thinking about their next fishing trips as the comforting aroma of the Spigworth village bonfire smoke filled the atmosphere.

Walter Wigmore and Squirt were happy with their day regardless of the lack of big fish, they had bigger fish to fry, or rather someone would be frying the fish for them at the local fish and chip shop in Lambert Lane.

Badger went home satisfied that his results had proven him right.

Will, Jed and Rick packed up their carp tackle and went to the pub again to encourage more hangovers, not a good idea as it was football the following morning.

Mark Gosling went home with thoughts of his next tench session in his head… even if you can't catch them in winter!

CHAPTER 8

A CHRISTMAS CARP

December started wet and miserable, not the most exciting or inspiring weather to go fishing. However, many anglers still ventured out despite the weather conditions. The rain had to stop sometime surely!

By mid December, the rain had stopped and a period of settled, if cloudy, weather prevailed.

Three anglers who fished on regardless of the climatic conditions were Jed Cleminson, Will Spring and Rick Western. A mere thing such as weather conditions could never thwart their insatiable desire to catch cyprinus carpio, except for thick ice on a frozen pond, but then only just! Rick Western was famous for taking a brace, bit and a saw with him in the January of 1969, just to wet his line. The 6-inch thick ice had formed on very calm water and was glass clear in certain areas; clear enough to see fish swimming underneath. In those days, Rick hadn't caught the carp bug and roach were his main target. The villagers were astounded to see Rick skimming along on ice skates with his fishing tackle and tools to make a hole in the ice.

After a bit of slipping up and falling over a few times, much to the enjoyment of the spectators, Rick managed to cut a 3 feet diameter hole in the ice.

Rick dispensed with his usual float rod and employed an 'ice hole fishing rod', which he had made from one of his old solid fibreglass fishing rods that he had broken years before. Circa 1975, there was a massive and irritating 'As Seen on TV' marketing campaign by the

Ronco company with their Pocket Fisherman. This little device, which was a short and stumpy fishing rod with its own inbuilt fishing reel, could be bought from all sorts of retailers; i.e. F W Woolworth, W H Smith, Boot's and Timothy White's etc. One could buy it from just about anywhere, anywhere that is apart from serious fishing tackle shops. I am certain that the Inuit folk weren't affected by this little contraption, they have been ice hole fishing for years so why fix something that isn't broken!

Rick was quite successful with his ice hole fishing, but he was later to find out just how successful by the end of the day.

It was four 'o clock in the afternoon, and the winter sky was as red as a blood orange. Thin ice was forming around the perimeter of the hole that Rick had cut; his fishing line was freezing and sticking to the rod rings on his rod. Rick decided to place his rod down on the ice to roll a cigarette, which wasn't the easiest of tasks with numb hands. As he lit the poorly folded sausage of tobacco and paper, Rick saw his float vanish slowly; he knew that it couldn't be a roach. Picking his rod up to strike, Rick felt a solid resistance on the end of his line. The fish was pulling so hard that Rick had to play it with the rod pointing down in the water, as he feared that the line might break on the ice. Fortunately, for Rick, the fight only went on for about a minute or less, and a 3lb common carp rolled over into the grateful folds of his landing net.

This winter experience changed everything for Rick; a serious carp angler was born.

Was Rick a serious carp angler? Well if 'serious' means dressing up in women's clothing, wearing make up and mincing about on the banks of Spigworth Pond just to ward off other anglers, then serious he was!

Wednesday 24th December 1975 means Christmas Eve to most of us. However, for Jed Cleminson, Will Spring and Rick Western, it was the last day of carp fishing before they had to commit themselves to normality and share the festive season with their loved ones. They weren't really as selfish as one might perceive, all three men had already bought Christmas presents for their wives and family, unlike some anglers that leave it to the last moment to visit the town, begrudgingly packing up a fishing session earlier than normal. Wandering around Woolworth's in a grubby wax cotton jacket, muddy wellies and stinking of mackerel after a pike fishing session is not very conducive to persuading sales staff to help you decide which present to buy for your wife.

Jed, Will and Rick the camp carp anglers three, chose to fish in three adjacent swims and were all dressed up in their winter fishing gear. Their customized platform soled Wellington boots made by the cobbler's in Camden High Street called 'Whoops Sweetie!', had become useful after all the rain of early December, the mud on the banks of Spigworth Pond was 5 inches deep in stodginess. To keep warm, a sensible West German Army tank suit from the army surplus store would fit the bill. However, Jed, Will and Rick would never settle for anything too masculine, no matter how cold it was. Instead, they had a dressmaker in Carnaby Street run up some quilted, double lined jump suits for them. Ever original, all three men chose their fabric from places one wouldn't normally buy from, a draper's shop in

Spinfield town called Curtains, Blinds & Nets Unlimited Limited.

Rick's tank suit was made from a shiny cloth with a large floral design, Jed's tank suit material had a print of birds and butterflies that bore no similarity to any of God's creations, and Will found an unusually patterned cloth with leopard spots. To keep their heads warm, they all wore fur hats reminiscent of the type a Russian saucy temptress would wear in a James Bond film.

As very few anglers fished Spigworth Pond in the depths of winter, one may wonder whom they were trying to frighten off wearing these clothes. Maybe they just enjoyed tarting themselves up!

As it was the festive season, Jed, Will and Rick decorated their fishing umbrellas with baubles and tinsel. Each had a Christmas fairy mounted on top of the central cap of their umbrellas for an authentic touch.

All three carp anglers were using a new type of bait for the winter. Well not so much new, but borrowed!

Shortly after Badger Bill Parsons success with the Spigworth tench and a carp previously in November, Jed spied him buying a large quantity of tinned cat food in his local Key Markets store. To the uninitiated, it would seem nothing out of the ordinary to see someone with a shopping basket brimming with tins of cat food. For Jed, it was a dead giveaway. Jed knew that Bill didn't own a cat as he was allergic to them. Jed had a flashback to that horrible lager induced hangover that November morning, and that puke provoking putrid pong that he caught a whiff of whilst talking to Badger about the carp he had caught. The memory of it still it turned his stomach.

The penny dropped and Jed sussed that Badger had been using tinned cat food as paste bait.

And so, with heaving shoulders of stifled retching, Jed set about making a paste bait of cat food mixed with plain wheat flour. The plan was to feed this concoction into the pond daily in small amounts so as not to over feed the carp but give them a taste for it. Will and Rick decided to undergo the same torture to capitalize on the bait campaign. With luck, this would encourage the carp to accept cat food as a natural source of nutrition.

It is unlikely though that carp would consider any unusual food as natural. They are, by nature, programmed to feed on nature's larder. The attraction and appeal of sticking ones head into five inches or deeper of black stinking silt to root out worms and wrigglers is too great.

However, any carp that has its head screwed on the right way, would know that it is better to expend less energy during the coldwater months and get all the nutrition they need in one mouthful, rather than digging about for small stuff. Perhaps then, the little stinky balls of cat food paste would do the trick for one of these intrepid carp anglers!

During this fishing session, Rick broke the news to Will and Jed that he had applied for a new job and won the position as a sales rep for an electric typewriter company called Speedy Secretary. He would start the training for the job locally in the early part of the New Year. A sales representative job was obviously not a static one, and involved driving around the country trying to sell typewriters, ribbons and correction fluid, this position would come into full effect during the 1976 coarse fishing close season. It was with much regret for Rick that his fishing time at Spigworth would be limited.

He would often be staying overnight in various B&B establishments when he had to visit customers in certain regions over a number of days. Worse still, he was going to wear his haircut short.

"Ooh luvvy! Not your lovely hair!" said Will.

"Never mind sweetie, we'll get you a nice wig!" Jed assured Rick.

"Thanks Jed, but I think I'll give it a miss." said Rick

"I'll have your Max Factor stuff Rick!" said Will.

"No, I think I'll hold onto it for old time's sake." answered Rick.

The mood of the day darkened slightly for Jed, Will and Rick as the thought of a dissolution of the glam piscatorial triad became a horrid reality. However, as this was going to be the last Christmas that they would fish together as femme fatales, a big booze up was in order.

They decided to leave their cars behind, lock their tackle away in the boat shed and book a taxi home when they had finished their fishing session.

Rick went off to get some supplies, Babycham and Brandy would be the perfect poison, and some bridge rolls and tins of hotdog sausages to soak it all up.

In the afternoon, Jed, Will and Rick, already woozy with Brandy and Babycham, reflected on the good times that they had together.

They talked about how they met during an S.C.A.C. AGM, 1971 in Frapham village hall. Of course, they knew of each other, as they had spoken in passing as anglers do. However, their connection of course was carp, as many anglers didn't have the time or inclination to cast a bait out and wait forever to get a bite, they became a carp angling clique.

They recalled how they overheard a conversation between two anglers with greasy DA haircuts while they were getting drinks at the bar, they were moaning about a 'fairy' they had seen on Top of the Pops. The fairy they were referring to was Marc Bolan, one of them referred to him as 'that curly haired git called T.REX!'

It occurred to Jed, Will and Rick that a majority of anglers were very masculine, or at least liked people to perceive them as masculine. It does seem odd that such a gentle sport, art or pastime, whatever one prefers to call it, would seem so fuelled with testosterone.

Many years later of course, it would be commonplace to see a burly carp angler in a t-shirt, jogging pants and brutally shorn hair, getting out of a white van. With knuckles trailing on the ground, dangling from heavily and badly tattooed arms that look as though he has had a nasty accident with a pack of permanent marker pens. The tattoos perhaps, dedicated to 'SHARON' or 'SHAZZA', just to get the point over that he likes girls and he is a MAN! Some of these white van carpers would wear the expression of 'I'm gonna beat you up if you talk to me!' to put your everyday friendly angler off from bothering them. Please don't ask them if they have caught anything when they haven't had a single bite all night? What a complete contrast to Jed, Will and Rick.

The conversation between the two 'dyed in the wool Teddy Boys' at the AGM was an inspiration to our Jed, Will and Rick. "What a great way of clearing Spigworth Pond of Neanderthal men!" they all agreed.

At first, it was just a little bit of eyeliner and mascara, but this later progressed to eye shadow, lipstick, foundation cream and rouge. It was common to hear

"Can I borrow your lippy sweetie?" or "That Boot's mascara really makes my eyes sore!" from those boys.

This passive approach to angler alienation had a devastating effect.

Shocked, concerned and downright prejudiced anglers wrote letters and made telephone calls of complaint to club secretary Bill Wilton. They asked him to put a stop to all this 'Nancy Boy' malarkey! However, Bill said that it would be difficult to apply a ban to Jed, Will and Rick glamming it up just because other people didn't like it.

Bill was adamant that he would not be making an addendum to the already strict club rules and byelaws; neither did he think a committee meeting broaching the subject would be effective. It would be difficult even in those days to justify a rule in a fishing club handbook that said…'No anglers should be seen to wear women's clothes or makeup on club waters unless they are a women.' Not only that, it could make the club look like a right bunch of Charlies and a complete laughing-stock!

Bill also appreciated the hard work that Jed, Will and Rick put into every close season work parties; Bill also knew the real reason behind their makeup!

At one time though, Jed did get an official warning when he pinched Antique Bluey's bottom for a bit of fun. Even then, poor Bill Wilton couldn't keep a straight face when he was reprimanding Jed during the disciplinary meeting.

"Now Mr Cleminson, I understand that Mr Bluet was occupying the swim you wanted to fish in, however, tweaking a person's buttock between thumb and forefinger to obtain the swim you want to fish in is not an acceptable practice…" At this point both Bill and Jed creased up with laughter and soon ended up rolling about on the floor in hysterics.

It was with deep regret for Jed that he never apologised personally to Laurie Bluet before he passed away at the end of September 1975. One should never leave things undone, we are not here for long, so better to fix things before we are gone.

The afternoon melted into dusk and the air temperature dropped rapidly. Not that Jed, Will and Rick had noticed it getting cold after drinking so much Brandy and Babycham. It was time to light the stove and get the hotdog sausages going.

"It's a shame you didn't buy any onions Rick, I could have fried them up to put in with hotdogs." said Will with melancholy.

"I wonder if Charlie Chatswell has got any onions he could give us?" said Rick.

"I think he keeps them in a sack in his outside toilet behind the pub." said Jed.

"I'll go and get some from there then, I won't bother Charlie as he's probably watching the telly." said Will.

"Yeah, he won't miss a few onions, you can tell him next time you go in for a pint." said Rick.

Opposite the entrance gate to Spigworth Pond was a wooden stile to climb over to the rear garden of the pub, much more convenient than trying to squeeze through the barbed wire fence and far less tank suit ripping.

Hopping over the wooden stile, Will made his way in the failing light to Charlie Chatswell's outside W.C. to borrow a few onions. In the toilet, he found two sacks of various sized onions. Not being fussy, Will took two big ones and returned to Jed and Rick.

At this point, Charlie Chatswell opened his back door to allow his newly acquired Rottweiler dog to go out for a tiddle; he had inherited the beast from an old aunty who was unable to look after it anymore.

The Rottweiler objected to Will the intruder and ran after him in hot pursuit.

Will suddenly became aware of heavy footfalls from a very heavy and angry beast. Looking behind and seeing a great dark shape making for him, Will ran to the stile. He just about made it over the stile, but not without the great dog biting and tearing a heel from one of his platform Wellington boots.

Will limped his way back to Jed and Rick, one heeled and feeling very sorry for himself.

With tinned frankfurter sausages and fried onions in fresh bridge rolls, life seemed as good as it could get, it got slightly better for all three carp anglers when Jed remembered that he had a bottle of scotch that he'd won in the Christmas raffle at work in the boot of his car.

By 8:00pm, the old BB adage 'be quiet and go a angling' had been completely forgotten as the cold, still, winter night air reverberated with loud cackling and loutish laughter from three young men who had also forgotten their ladylike manners.

The disco held in the Shepherd and Crook that Christmas Eve was almost as loud, one could clearly hear the strains of a very happy pub clientele singing along to the Christmas number one hit Bohemian Rhapsody by Queen. What else could an inebriated trio of carp anglers in drag do but join in, even if badly!

Without going into too much detail, the operatic section of Bohemian Rhapsody was not for sore ears,

Jeds's rendering of Roger Taylor's part of 'Galileo' was halted when something tickled his throat and made him cough violently and eventually throw up. What jolly japes the three camp carpers were having!

The music from the pub silenced suddenly when an untimely electrical power failure interrupted the proceedings. Most likely, the power failure was due to TV watchers draining the electricity supply of the village as they tuned into a feature length film on BBC1 of the incredibly popular Kojak.

Loud drunken jeers followed, as Charlie made a frantic search for candles. There hadn't been any need to use candles since the 1973 power cuts, when British coal miners decided to work-to-rule and fuel was in short supply. Why were there always power cuts when there was something good to watch on television?

Charlie finally found the candles to cheers and a round of applause and then went out to the back of the pub to kick the oil-powered generator into action. The disco was back in full swing and Christmas Eve was fast becoming Christmas Day.

When their raucous singing subsided, Jed, Will and Rick started to talk about the Spinfield Coarse Angling Club and its members.

"What do you two think of Walter Wigmore?" asked Jed.

"He's alright I suppose, apart from the way he dresses." said Rick.

"Yes, the trilby and demob suit is a bit passé isn't it sweetie!" agreed Will

"No, I meant what do you think of Walter as an angler?" asked Jed again.

"Yeah, it's strange isn't it, he seems to do everything right but doesn't have a great deal of luck." said Rick.

"He's definitely eccentric though isn't he." said Will.

"I suppose you have to be, to be an angler." said Jed.

"Not that we're eccentric of course." Rick assured himself.

"No, we're only pretending!" laughed Will.

"What about Mark Gosling?" asked Rick.

"Now he is odd!" said Will.

"He never seems very happy, he must have had a sad life." said Rick.

"I guess some people are afraid to show their softer side." said Jed.

"Yeah, but some store it all up until it finally explodes." said Rick.

"Yes, we missed that at the beginning of the season didn't we? Apparently he turned blue because he was laughing so hard." said Will.

"Apparently Squirt ran to the phone box to call for an ambulance, he may well have saved Mark's life." said Rick.

"Mark doesn't seem to hold much regard for Squirt though, it makes you wonder why Squirt even bothers to be chummy with him." said Will.

"I think it's the father figure thing, I don't remember much about Squirt at school apart from that his clothes were always dirty and he smelled." said Jed.

Jed added that he remembered Squirt coming to school with a black eye or two now and again and it was rumoured that his dad used to beat him after he came home from the pub.

"Still, he seems to be mates with old Wiggy Wigmore these days, so maybe he has found a real friend." said Rick.

"Yes, some people have sad lives, but sometimes things seem to turn out alright for them eventually." Jed sighed.

"He's still an annoying git though!" laughed Will.

The disco music in The Shepherd and Crook was getting louder, so was the clientele, singing loudly to the chorus of That's The Way (I Like It) by KC and the Sunshine Band.

It was 10:30pm and no fighting had started yet, which was unusual because proprietor Bernie Burns of The Pheasant pub a quarter mile away would normally throw his regulars out by 10:00pm once they became too rowdy! From there, they would stagger to The Shepherd and Crook to cause trouble. However, that particular year Charlie Chatswell had hired two burly door attendants to turn away anyone who didn't have tickets for the Christmas disco. The disco had always been a ticketed event but had problems with gatecrashers in the past.

Unfortunately, after the yobs received short shrift from the bouncers, the trouble diverted elsewhere. Jed noticed an orange glow near the roadside swims. Shortly after, the sound of fire engine sirens caused excitement. Jed, Will and Rick went to investigate.

On arrival at the scene, it became painfully clear to Rick that some vandals in their Christmas excitement had smashed a window and set his car alight!

With his spirits low, Rick shrugged his shoulders and said "Come on girls; let's get back to our rods?"

"That's a bit of bad luck Rick." said Will.

"Yeah, I hope your insurance will cover the damage enough to get another car." said Jed.

"I don't give a damn about the bloody car; it's the sassy pair of stilettos in the boot I'm upset about!" Rick retorted sharply.

"Ooh lover, that's terrible." said Jed.

"Ah shut up you silly old queen!" said Rick.

Realising the comedy behind the irony, all three carp anglers burst into fits of hysterical laughter. They had played their parts as transvestites so convincingly; they had started to believe it themselves.

They returned to their fishing pitches.

Settling back in their swims, with a few more nips of scotch imbibed, the anglers became silent and contemplative.

"Anyone fancy a spliff?" asked Rick.

"Why, have you got some then?" answered Will with a question.

"No, I just wondered if anyone fancied a spliff, that's all." said Rick.

"What's the time?" asked Jed.

"It's a quarter past eleven." said Will, the only one there with luminous hands on his watch.

"I think I'll reel in at midnight." said Jed.

"Yeah, me too." agreed Will.

"We haven't had a single bite and yet I've enjoyed this session almost as much as some of our best." said Rick.

"Yes well it's not all about catching fish is it!" proclaimed Jed.

"No it isn't." agreed Rick.

Although the goal of any angler is to catch fish, there are times when an angler doesn't catch anything but is nonetheless glad to have been by the side of a pond, canal or river; it just helps if you do catch something!

The three carp anglers sat quietly, listening to the sounds of Christmas Eve. Distant drunken male voices shouting to each other, even though they were only across the road. Angry mothers frustrated after hours of trying to get their excited children to sleep, to find them woken up by the noisy blighters in the street.

"Mum, is it Christmas Day yet?"

"No, go back to sleep or Father Christmas won't leave your presents!"

"But it's light outside!"

"It's the full moon, now go back to sleep!"

Some drunks would go home to bed or watch whatever was left of the television until closedown. Alternatively, fall asleep before closedown, to wake up later with the television screen blank and a high-pitched signal emanating from the speaker.

Every reveller would awake to a magical holiday, the only time off from work that they could take without feeling guilty for letting their employers down as everyone else was having that same time off as well.

Of course, the odd reveller will wake up with the worst hangover and stomach upset of their lives, vowing never do it again, until next Christmas at least!

At ten minutes to midnight, Jed said that he was going to start packing his fishing gear up.

Rick shouted, "No don't pack up yet, it's not over until midnight!"

"I must admit that I don't think we're going to catch anything in the next ten minutes or so." said Will.

"No, give it 'til midnight and then we'll reel in and get that taxi!" asserted Rick.

"Well, I'm going to start packing up most of my stuff and leave the rods and landing net out until last." said Jed.

"That isn't a bad idea actually, at least we won't have much more to pack away then." concurred Will.

Suddenly, out in front of Rick's swim, there was the sound of a caudal fin flapping, and a huge crash as a carp leapt and belly flopped back into the pond.

"I'm not reeling in, this one's going to be mine!" said Rick excitedly.

"We're all using the same bait, it could equally be my fish." said Jed.

"What, are you going to stay here all night?" asked Will.

"I won't need to, I've just got a feeling that I'm going to get a bite in a moment." replied Rick with certainty.

The next few minutes crawled like an earthworm on a hot pavement slab, attempting to make its way to some moist soil before the Sun dehydrates its delicate body. Why do worms do that?

At midnight, the bells of Frapham church rang out their song for midnight mass, which was something else to irk the mothers of the village as their children woke once again.

This midnight campanology was impromptu and not the norm for Frapham church at Christmas, or any other time of year. The campanologist culprits were five louts from Spigworth village, who had managed to find a stash of communion wine in the vestry to soak up. In celebration of the festive season, they chose to ring in Christmas day in style.

The five horrors were quickly despatched with a very painful flee in their ears by 'man of the cloth' and ex pugilist instructor for the Frapham village hall youth club, the Reverend Thomas Pilcher.

While this unusual act of Yuletidery was going on, Rick was completely oblivious to his reel handle spinning backwards as a large carp bolted off in panic after picking up the wrong piece of cat food paste.

"What's that whirring noise?" said Will.

Rick looked down at one of his rods and realised that the noise was coming from his fishing reel. Somehow, Rick had forgotten to turn his electronic bite alarm on.

With no further ado, Rick grabbed his rod and struck into the running fish.

"It's on!" shouted Rick.

The fish tore off into the darkness, forcing Rick to back-wind with his reel rapidly as the fish stole yards and yards of fishing line.

Ever since his encounter in Greenies Number 9 at the beginning of the season, Rick preferred to play fish with the reel handle rather than the slipping clutch in the reel spool, he felt that he had more control over the fish. Certainly, the common noise of anglers enjoying the loud buzz of the clutch, just to let other anglers know that they had caught something, annoyed him. At least if a fish was heading toward snags, and undoubtedly freedom, he could clamp down on the reel handle to slow the fish down and possibly turn it away from the snags without fiddling about with the adjustable drag on the front of the spool. Let's face it, if you allow a carp to head merrily on into overhanging tree branches dangling in the water, you're going to lose it whatever. So better to try to stop the fish in its tracks. If it comes off, it wasn't your fish that day anyway!

Eventually, Rick began to gain more control on the fish, winning line back, yard by yard. The carp was close in to the bank.

"It's nearly played out." said Rick as he fumbled around in his pockets for a small torch with his left hand.

Rick located his torch in a right-hand pocket and cursed his stupidity for not making the torch easily accessible in a left hand pocket. Holding the rod with a hulking great carp surging away on the end of the line, with his left arm across his middle as he fiddled about for a torch in the right pocket, did not make the playing of the fish easy!

Rick flicked the torch on and held it between his teeth to get a better idea of where the fish was in the close vicinity. Grabbing for the landing net and gently introducing it into the water, Rick caught sight of his prize. Unfortunately, the carp caught sight of the landing net and bolted off again for a short distance, but the fish's fight was all but over, only the hook popping out of its lip could save it!

The characters of carp vary so much in playing them, most give some sort of account for themselves. Some carp will fight to the very last and thrash about in the landing net and on the bank. While at the other end of the spectrum, you can catch the odd carp that appears to know the routine, does a bit of flapping around just to go through the motions, willingly gliding into the folds of the net, and going through the weighing and photo shoot ceremony without fuss. The latter will often swim off strongly on return to the water, possibly thinking, "Damn it! I slipped up there, of all the tasty morsels I had to pick up it had to be that one!" That's if fish think and talk to themselves of course!

Rick's carp was slowly weakening and soon found itself being pulled on its side over the landing net.

With the carp safely in the net, Rick collapsed the landing net arms and drew them together to pull the fish out of the water and gently place it on the bank for unhooking.

The hook had already dropped out in the net; Rick breathed a sigh of relief that the hook hadn't come adrift before the fish had been landed.

In the torchlight, Rick noticed a characteristic black spot on the carp's heard, it was 'Fatso'! The fish that old Greenie had been trying to catch before he died, and the carp that Rick landed on Greenie's rod at the beginning of the season.

This time though, Fatso looked even fatter. On weighing the carp, the scales tipped at a little over 38lbs 4oz.

"If I hadn't had so much booze to drink today, I'd be sinking another to celebrate." said Will.

"Cor yeah, I'm scared of waking up tomorrow morning, I reckon my head will be banging." said Jed.

"Yes, I think I'll give it a miss myself." agreed Rick.

With Fatso returned safely to her home in Spigworth Pond, Jed, Will and Rick packed away their tackle in the club boatshed for the last time as the glam trio.

The three men stood silently at the roadside as they waited for the taxi that had been booked to take them home.

Much later, a black Hackney cab turned up to collect them.

Unfortunately, the taxi driver was one of the Marc Bolan hating Teddy Boys that Jed, Will and Rick had overheard talking at the 1971 AGM in Frapham village hall.

The taxi driver took one look at the three heavily made up men and shouted, "YOU CAN BOOK ANOTHER TAXI RANK, I AIN'T TAKING A BUNCH OF NANCIES 'OME!"

The taxi driver drove off as though he had the hounds of Hades biting at his buttocks!

"Oh that's great! What are we going to do now?" said Jed in desperation.

"I think we'll have to walk." said Rick.

"Oh yeah, that will be great, me limping home with a busted heel on my boot!" exclaimed Will.

"Why, you didn't drive here with those great big poofy boots on did you?" asked Rick.

"Oh no, that's true, I've got some shoes in the car!" remembered Will.

At that moment, a Morris Mini Traveller drew up and the driver wound down the passenger to speak to the three men, a strong whiff of Chanel No 5 wafted out of the car.

"Ooh 'allo you bunch of lovelies! Fancy a lift?"

It was Cheryl the transvestite, the person that Jed had the uncertain pleasure to meet in August.

"Err, no thanks mate, we're waiting for a taxi." said Jed in his best 'I'm a bloke and I like football and boxing' masculine voice.

"Alright, suit yourself then love, Happy Christmas, bye!" said Cheryl with a cheery wave as he drove off.

"What did you have to go and say that for you steaming great twit?" asked Rick.

"Well, he makes me feel uneasy with all that dragging up." said Jed defensively.

"WHAT?????" said Rick and Will in unison.

"Take a look at yourself Jed, you're hardly dressed as a bricklayer now are you!" said Rick.

"Yeah, hypocrite!" jeered Will.

"Alright, alright! Maybe I was a little harsh." said Jed.

"Anyway, whatever, it looks as though were going on Shanks's Pony now!" moaned Rick.

"Come on girls, let's walk?" said Will.

Will changed into his shoes and the camp carpers three made their way home on foot.

Jed, Will and Rick had only walked a couple of hundred yards up the road, when a car slowly pulled up to halt just in front of them.

"Hello lads, need a lift home?" asked a kindly voice in the dark.

They approached the driver with consternation.

Instead of the homophobic, psychotic killer with a penchant for men wearing makeup they had expected, the driver was lovely old Walter Wigmore.

Walter had just dropped his sister Wilhelmina off home after they had been to a Christmas dance at Spinfield Assembly Hall and was on his way home himself.

"Oh thank you Walter!" said Rick with relief.

Walter drove the men home to their doors and waited for each one to go in and make sure they got indoors safely. Why can't all people be kind like that?

That was the last time that Jed, Will and Rick wore makeup and feminine clothes.

Rick pursued his career as a typewriter sales representative, only occasionally fishing on Spigworth Pond when he had time off.

Will and Jed continued to fish together, though not at Spigworth, it didn't seem right without Rick.

But, one thing Jed, Will and Rick always held dear in their memories was the companionship and the giggles as they frightened off anglers with their cheeky camp ways…oh, and a little bit of carp fishing now and then!

CHAPTER 9

FOR AULD LANG SYNE

It was Thursday 1st January 1976, and another plague of hangovers were re-enacted by those who vowed 'never again' on Christmas Day 1975. Little wonder the British Government made New Year's Day a Bank Holiday in 1974, with all those soreheads every 1st of January there was no point in opening for business. I would like to point out though, as the author of this tome which I am pleased you have read this far, I clearly remember having to work in a factory on New Year's Day in 1978. Obviously, some companies took no notice of this government standard.

At the beginning of 1976, the rock band Queen was still at number 1 in the UK Hit Parade with Bohemian Rhapsody. Queen's regal reign came to end when a Swedish Quartet named ABBA with their song Mama Mia dethroned them. This Scandinavian phenomenon captured the British imaginations on the 6th of April 1974 by blowing all the contestants off stage at the Brighton Dome by winning the Eurovision Song Contest. Agnetha, Björn, Benny and Anni-Frid would go on to dominate the UK charts with their catchy songs for the next year, and include two other number one hits Fernando and Dancing Queen.

So what has all this to do with Spigworth Pond in 1976? Nothing really, I just thought you might like to know!

The start of the New Year at Spigworth weather wise was unremarkable. There was no snow to talk of; ironically, it did eventually snow freakily on June 2nd. Apparently, the Derbyshire versus Lancashire County Cricket Match was interrupted due to lack of visibility, although the little white flakes didn't settle because the ground was too warm.

There would be little rain in 1976 either, many reservoirs, lakes and ponds virtually drying out. When the rain did eventually come in September, swollen rivers flooded many plains where the earth was too dry to soak it all up.

The summer itself would be a heat wave, record temperatures reaching 35.6°C in Southampton, inspiring a regional television weather forecaster to fry an egg on a paving slab just to prove the point.

With this heat wave, just to make things a little more unbearable, there were squadrons of giant ladybirds. There were reports of the ladybirds landing on people and giving them a nasty nip. To call it an infestation would be an understatement, it would have been more appropriate to call it an epidemic. It was almost impossible to walk anywhere on solid ground without the sound and sensation of red shells with black spots crunching underfoot. It was bad news for people that enjoyed walking barefoot, it was also bad news for any self respecting greenfly that summer!

The anglers of the S.C.A.C that were fortunate enough to avoid being pickled on New Year's Eve 1975 were few, but predictably on the first day of 1976, Walter Wigmore took advantage of any time that God gave him to go fishing.

When one falls in love with a body of water that one enjoys fishing, there can't be many more joyous scenarios than to find oneself completely and selfishly alone by that same body of water. Walter Wigmore found himself in this divine situation.

It was a reasonably cold day, overcast and 6°C with a force 4 North East wind.

Walter chose to fish swim number 10, not for any particular reason other than he felt comfortable there. Number 10 was also the swim that Walter proudly caught his big tench earlier in the season. It was also a good swim because, with the dead bankside reeds lying flat, Walter could virtually see the entire pond, so he could observe any signs of fish movement and move swims if action proved to be slow.

His current friend and fishing partner Peter 'Squirt' Burt was absent that day, he had unfortunately been ill with diarrhoea and sickness over the festive season and was still feeling a bit ragged. I'm sure you feel enriched with that knowledge!

One of the great things about the festive season is that anglers often receive angling related gifts; Walter was one of those lucky anglers.

His wife bought him a lovely new hollow glass pike rod, mail ordered from specialist tackle dealer Jimmy's of Bundleton. The pike rod, an 11ft two-piece 3lb test curve beast, was of a limited edition hand made and signed by rod builder Leonard Hithertoe. Matched with a Mitchell 810 fixed spool reel, Walter was the bee's knees.

Walter didn't want to restrict himself to pike fishing that day, he had also taken a light float rod with him to catch tiddlers. It is amazing how much a few little roach caught on a float-fished maggot can ease the hardship of a cold and otherwise biteless day.

Whilst setting up his pike rod and tackle, Walter became aware of an explosion of small roach dispersing as a predator terrorised them close to the near bankside reeds. This seemed a good a place as any for Walter to cast a sprat.

With a gentle flick, the sprat plopped into the water and something took it immediately, taking his little bung float with it. The line tightened as Walter clicked the bale arm of his reel with a loud CLUNK! After a short and spirited fight, a little jack pike of just over 2lbs flapped about in Walter's landing net.

"Well, if I catch nothing else today, at least I can say I have caught the species that I came to catch." thought Walter.

The fishing was very slow for Walter that day, and as most anglers do, he drifted off into thoughts of the past, when times were warmer and kinder.

Walter's mind went back to his childhood. The school summer holiday August 1947, when his parents took him for a walk on Spinfield Pier one warm and humid evening. He could still smell the smells of the food stalls, with hot dogs, candyfloss and shellfish. Ugh! He remembered eating his first punnet of winkles, fiddling about with a pin to get the little mollusc out of its shell, and the chewiness of its flesh and the crunchiness of sand between his teeth.

He remembered the noises of people enjoying themselves and the ringing of bells in the amusements arcade, and the fight that broke out when someone had won the jackpot on the one-arm bandit.

"Oi, you! That's my money you've just won there pal!"

"No it ain't, I won it fair and square!"

"I been loadin' that machine up all afternoon, and you comes along and sticks yer bloomin' penny in and wins the lot!"

"That's the whole point of the game you idiot!"

"Don't you call me an idiot, take that!" (The perfect punch on the nose)

"Ow, me nose is bleedin'!"

The intervention of the amusement arcade manager:-

"Awright, awright lads, pack it in before someone gets badly hurt!"

"Yah shaddup you fat old git!"

Another perfect punch on the amusement arcade manager's nose:-

"Oof, right that's it I'm callin' the police!"

All the time this was going on, opportunists filled their pockets with the pennies that had overflowed on the floor. When the police finally came to the rescue, announced by the loud, proud tinkle telltale of bells on their car, the fight was over and the spectators had dispersed as though nothing had happened. The only evidence left over from the brawl was a few nosey drips of blood on the wooden deck.

Walter remembered something else about that balmy evening stroll on the pier, the evening he fell in love with fishing.

As Walter and his parents walked to the end of the pier, they came across four men fishing.

There was a sudden burst of excitement as one of the angler's split cane rod tip frantically bounced up and down. We call it a bite, but it is really an indication of an angry and frightened fish already hooked tugging away on the end of the line.

After a few puffs of cigarette smoke and a bit of swearing emanating from the angler's mouth, a drop-net was lowered in to the sea by one of the other anglers to cradle a lovely bass. This fish was the most silvery and wonderfully huge fish Walter had ever seen. From that moment on, Walter knew what he wanted to do for the rest of his life.

Walter pled with his parents to buy him a fishing rod and reel, but his parents were too poor to buy anything like that, and told Walter regrettably that he would have to wait until he was old enough to get a paper round job to buy one himself.

However, one Saturday morning Walter's father bought a pair of long bamboo canes from a hardware store, and some hooks, fine silk line, split lead shot and tiny crow's quill floats from a little tackle shop opposite Spinfield Pier.

"What do you think these are Walter?" said his father laying the bamboo canes down on the kitchen table.

"They're bamboo canes for growing runner beans up." Walter replied.

"That's right." said Walter's father.

Walter's father fumbled about in his jacket pocket and pulled out a brown paper bag containing the spool of fishing line, hooks float and lead shot.

Walter's father, emptying the contents of the paper bag onto the kitchen table asked, "What do these bits, and the bamboo canes make together?"

"I don't know daddy, is it something to do with gardening?" asked Walter with excitement.

"If I tie some of this silk thread onto the thin end of the cane, and then tie a hook onto the other end of the silk, what do you think I could do with it?" quizzed Walter's father.

"It's a fishing rod!" said Walter jumping up and down excitedly, followed by a quick dash outdoors to the WC before he wet himself.

Later on in the early evening, after digging the garden for some earthworms, Walter's father took him on a long walk with the improvised fishing tackle. The walk, although only half an hour long seemed like forever to Walter, when you don't know where you are going, time seems to slow down.

After crossing a very busy main road, the Wigmore anglers climbed over a wooden stile and walked a public footpath through three fields of golden wheat, not yet harvested. The wheat was almost as tall as Walter, which he found quite unnerving. Walter's father pointed out a field mouse that had managed to climb to the top of a wheat stalk to dine on the wheat kernels. Walter was interested, but nonetheless, eager to get to the end of the spooky walk through the crops.

Eventually, the Wigmores arrived at a barn by Southbrook Farm; by the barn was a little pond about sixty feet long and 50 feet wide.

A moorhen swam away in panic with jerking head to the far bank under an overhanging willow frond. The air was full of farmyard and pond-life aromas that Walter would remember forever; these pongs would always remind him of that first fishing trip with his father.

After tying some line to the bamboo canes, Walter's father took out a pamphlet, given free of charge from the tackle shop owner with any purchase of tackle. The point of the pamphlet was to instruct novice anglers how to set up their terminal tackle. The pamphlet also demonstrated more importantly, the correct knots to tie hooks on properly. The fishing tackle shop owner grew tired of angler's complaining that the hooks he sold them were rubbish because they kept coming off whenever they caught a fish, so the free pamphlet was his perfect disclaimer.

The little Southbrook Farm pond was quite shallow with the deepest part being a three feet deep hole under a tree at the north end. The pond contained mostly three spined sticklebacks; it was brimming with them in fact.

After rigging both canes up with floats, shot, hooks with the all important finishing touch, small wriggling worms, the Wigmore boys were ready to do battle with the Leviathan, all be it of a quite small three spined variety.

It was exciting for Walter, as soon as he plopped his worm bait in the water, his little crow's quill float bobbed about and travelled slowly across the surface of the pond as it was towed by a wrestling stickleback with an insatiable appetite for little brown worms. In reality, underneath the surface of the pond the stickleback was quite concerned, as it had committed itself to swallow something that was as long as its own body. The little fish's eyes rolled about as its pectoral fins waved frantically, it was hard to take in oxygen with that dirty great python blocking the gills.

Then suddenly, the stickleback's world went slightly crazier as it found itself dragged skyward and finally suspended in mid air, dangling from a length of silken thread. There was actually no need for hooks other than to attach the worm to the end of the line; the sticklebacks didn't even get as far as getting the hook in, all that was needed was to pull the worm out of the tiddler's mouth. Walter could have used the same worm all day for those little fish!

As exciting as it was swinging in those little dark green and silver treasures one after the other, Walter's sense of adventure became stronger, he yearned to try something different. Walter decided to up-sticks to try fishing the deeper bit at the north end of the pond. One could fish the deeper hole from the bank at the side of the tree; Walter however, chose to become a true adventurer and crawled underneath the low overhanging branches to lean across another branch to drop his bait in. To Walter's amazement, his float sank away immediately and he was soon doing battle with a fish much bigger than the ones he had been catching.

"Dad! Dad! I've caught a really big stickleback!" Walter shouted.

Before Walter's father rose from his pitch there was a loud crack and splash as the branch Walter was leaning across snapped, plummeting the poor child into the depths.

Walter's father retrieved his stinking silt smothered sobbing son from the pond. Walter was still holding onto the bamboo cane and the giant stickleback was still thrashing about on the end of the line, when Walter realised this, all the crying stopped.

It wasn't a stickleback at all, it was a perch no bigger than a couple of ounces in weight. To Walter though, it was his first proper coarse fish and he was ready to conquer the world of freshwater fishing.

Mrs Wigmore reprimanded both boys severely when they returned home. Mrs Wigmore chastised Mr Wigmore for not looking after Walter, and she rebuked Walter for making his clothes filthy and being so stupid.

Mr Baldwin, the Wigmore's next-door neighbour soon learned of Walter's interest in all things piscatorial. Mr

Baldwin dusted off an old case that he had kept on a shelf in his shed for many years; the case contained a traveller's fishing set once owned by his elder brother. Tragically, his brother died from fatal wounds in the third battle of Ypres 5th November 1917, just before the fall of Passchendaele village,

Mr Baldwin presented the little case to a wide-eyed Walter who had absolutely no idea what was inside. Once Walter unfastened the brass catches of the little case, a musty aroma filled his nostrils. Inside the blue velvet lined case was a little wooden reel and six small 18 inch sections of bamboo that could be fitted together to make a fishing rod. The rod, although essentially a fly-fishing rod, had an additional screw-in butt section to convert it into a conventional rod. Mr Baldwin explained to Walter about the history and the sentiment behind the fishing set, and that the set was unique as it had been hand-made by his late brother. To say that Walter was elated would be an understatement, let us just say he got to the Moon before Neil Armstrong. Mr Baldwin gave Walter the page with the cartoon strip of Mr Crabtree Goes Fishing from the Daily Mirror regularly, Walter would cut them out and paste them into a scrapbook with flour paste, and enthusiasm.

Mr Crabtree would be a role model for Walter forever.

A swan swooped down crashing carelessly into Spigworth Pond, rousing Walter from his daydream and making waves of float unsettling annoyance. The swan swam to the far margins to dip its head into the shallows with hopes of food. A flapping of pheasant wings as it flew out from a nearby copse and a loud boom from a shotgun followed, spraying lead shot into the air, finally falling to the ground and into the margins of Spigworth Pond where the swan was feeding.

Within a decade from that moment, the British Government would outlaw the use of split lead shot in angling following the discovery that swan deaths were on the increase due to ingestion of the little balls of Plumbum.

The British Government didn't ban all lead in angling, size 6 shot up to 1oz weights were considered to be the most hazardous to swans, anything smaller or larger was not considered a problem.

Nevertheless, even before the lead ban came into force in1986, the angling trade had already been offering alternatives to the banned lead weights; the tackle manufacturers gave anglers the opportunity to adjust to the change before the ban.

One of the first alternatives (I won't say substitutes, because they were not) to lead shot were manufactured by the excellent Swedish tooling company Sandvik. Instead of the usual split in the shot to squeeze the fishing line between for mounting, the alternative had two semi spheres of a tungsten alloy with little soft copper hinges to emulate the split. They were quite useless, often flying off during a cast. However, at least the anglers could take comfort in the knowledge that they weren't poisoning the swans anymore, regardless of how many shot they were distributing into the water. Moreover, the manufacturer of these objectionable little beasts took comfort in the knowledge that they would be selling more and more of the shot alternatives as anglers frantically purchased enough to combat their losses, for a short time at least! Other versions of split shot emerged to improve the situation; some of them were so hard they could weaken the fishing line when compressed.

To have an alternative means one has a choice, when the lead ban came into force, there was no alternative, and one had to use what was available!

Walter searched the surface of the pond for the tip of his float after losing concentration, thanks to the shotgun blast. The float tip had disappeared!

Walter swept his float rod back into a strike; there was a certain amount of resistance on the end of his line. After a short battle, Walter drew a nice plump roach of around 12oz towards his landing net, only for a huge pike to swipe it at the last moment. Annoyingly, after a brief but frantic tussle, the pike won, leaving Walter and the roach separated forever.

Walter reeled in, sorted out the pike tooth damaged line, and set up his float rig again.

It was 10:00am and time for a cup of coffee from the thermos and a bite to eat. Walter had strawberry jam sandwiches and a chocolate bar. The chocolate bar, Fry's Five Boys*, his favourite, sent Walter's mind wandering back to another sweet time of his youth.

When Walter was 15 years of age, his parents gave him his first bicycle for his birthday to help him get about and to ride to his job in a local pharmaceutical sundry factory. He never did get that paper round due to the lack of wheels. This was a life changer for Walter. It was only a second hand bike, well not a second hand purchase exactly, Walter's father found it on the old bombsite not far from their home. Walter's father assumed the bicycle had been dumped, as the original owner had no further need for the velocipede; he rescued it for renovation.

The bicycle was very rusty, in fact the only metal part that wasn't corroded was the little brass badge on the steering column that boasted that the bike was indeed made by Royal Enfield.

After a fair bit of clanging, tinkering, Emery cloth rasping and swearing, the frame of the bicycle began to look more decent. Walter's father lovingly coated all the bare metal with two coats of red oxide paint as an undercoat. When the red oxide had dried, he over painted it with three coats of sky-blue gloss cellulose paint.

The chrome-plated parts such as the handlebars and wheel rims were severely corroded and flaking. But with a little more swearing, a damned good rub down with various grades of Emery cloth and the promise of a couple of pints in the Lion's Mane boozer down the road, Walter's father cajoled his mate Ronnie the electroplater to bring back the sparkle to the sad old steel.

All that the bicycle needed to complete it was some new spokes, tyres, inner tubes, a set of cycle lamps and a saddle. For the princely sum of 12/- 6d, a newish bike was reborn. He executed all of this hard work without Walter's knowledge.

Walter remembered his father bringing this brown paper, string wrapped and oddly shaped thing into the kitchen.

"I think you may find this is for you Walter." said Walter's father.

"What is it dad?" asked Walter.

"Well unwrap it and find out!" demanded his father.

Being careful so as not to damage the brown paper so that it may be re-used (this was not that long after the Second World War and folk were more frugal and less wasteful in those days!), Walter saw one of the most exciting things he had ever seen in his life.

Although this was Walter's first ever bike, he had learned to ride on his friend Freddy Winter's bicycle, Freddy allowed him to borrow it occasionally. This was Freddy's spare bicycle; his father was a bank manager and was able to afford to buy new things for his son, the spoilt brat!

There was a big difference with Walter's new cycle in comparison to the one he had learnt on; it had no brakes on the handlebars! This immediately panicked Walter, but his father showed him that the bicycle would slow down or stop by backpedalling, this bicycle had a coaster braking system in the hub of the rear wheel.

The bicycle opened up a new world of adventure for Walter; he cycled everywhere and made many discoveries. One of his discoveries was a little pond, five miles away near a village called Sawpot. The pond was in a wooded area called Deal Copse in a small estate called The Deal. The pond, less than a quarter of an acre in size, was virtually covered with lily pads throughout the summer. However, there were areas that were clear of lily pads where one could easily wet a line. This would be a place for Walter to fish, and best of all, it was free!

The cycle ride itself was arduous to say the least; Larkmore Lane was a mile long and uphill travelling north. There was one lung-emptying hill towards the end of the lane to encounter before everything levelled out to come as relief for tired legs. Most cyclists dismounted before that hill, to cowardly walk up to the top before remounting to ride the easier part. Walter was not a coward, he just got out of the saddle and stood up to pedal, it was much quicker than walking!

On the main road to Deal Pond, Walter passed a massive pond that wielded a threatening wooden sign with red lettering on a post. WARNING! KEEP OUT! PRIVATE! TRESPASSERS WILL BE PROSECUTED! This was Spigworth Pond prior to the Spinfield Coarse Angling Club securing rights to fish there.

Walter would go to fish Deal Pond most Saturdays, and a bar of the aforementioned Fry's Five Boys was always involved. On some warmer days, the little chocolate bar would melt and Walter resorted to licking the foil wrapper. It was less enjoyable than snapping a piece of the bar off and having a good old chomp, but waste not, want not!

Walter was still fishing with the handmade fishing set that his next-door neighbour gave him, and he enjoyed catching little tench and roach. Sometimes a little goldfish would turn up as well.

With one exception of a clearing to the estate lawn, woodland surrounded Deal Pond; wild fallow deer ran through the gaps in the trees with regularity. When Walter first encountered the deer in the half-light of the woodland, he was slightly frightened because he imagined they were pack dogs unleashed to intercept trespassers. He eventually grew used to seeing the fallow deer and worried no more; well, that was until an event that became indelibly imprinted in his memory. One late autumn afternoon, Walter heard a noise in the woods behind him that sounded like somebody kicking a metal bucket. Looking behind him, Walter saw a huge array of antlers; a fallow buck was looking at him. Walter froze with fear and looked away, hoping that the beast would flee. Suddenly there was a loud crack coming from the same direction, it was the same deer practicing a bit of rutting with another angry deer.

Walter soon realised that he need not fear them and carried on with his fishing.

In the clearing of the woods, was a large house owned by the Caesar family. In the front garden of the large house was a statue of an angel.

On a late summer evening, Walter was startled when a young girl appeared from the woods and asked him if he had caught any fish. The girl was Susan Caesar, 13 years of age and the youngest daughter of the family who owned the big house across the pond. Susan sat on the grass beside Walter and chatted to him for a while before her mother called her to go home. This wouldn't be the last time that Walter and Susan met, in fact Walter looked forward to their regular Deal Pond rendezvous' and would often share his Five Boys with her.

Susan was a beautiful little girl, a bit tomboyish, but very pretty. Walter would sit in conversation with Susan and gaze with wonderment at her gorgeous green eyes and shiny dark brown hair. Susan enjoyed eating sweets, liquorice torpedoes were her favourite. Susan's relish for this delicacy was extremely apparent, the surrounds of her lips were often coloured with the food dye used in the confection.

Then one Saturday evening it happened, Walter fell in love with Susan. It all came about after he had caught and landed a little tench and showed Susan how wonderful it was.

"Look Susan, isn't he lovely!" said Walter.

"Yes he is Walter!" replied Susan.

Walter returned the little tench with a little plop back into the water.

Suddenly, Susan grabbed hold of Walter in a passionate hug and said "Oh Walter, I think you're lovely too!" with a hint of liquorice on her breath, kissing him firmly on the lips.

Their lips became luxuriously, but sadly temporarily, adhered with the sticky sweet sugariness of liquorice torpedo lipstick. That moment stirred emotions and feelings inside that Walter had never known before.

I won't be any more explicit than that, come on now, we are all grown ups, and you know exactly what I mean! Behave yourselves! Suffice to say, Walter found it the most uncomfortable bicycle ride home ever.

The memory of Susan's baby soft face pressed against his, the taste of liquorice in Susan's kiss occupied his every thought and he wanted to live that moment forever.

This romance carried on for some weekends to come, until one Saturday when Walter arrived at Deal Pond to find the big house looking extremely deserted. The statue of the angel was also missing.

Susan's family had moved away to another county after her father had taken on a new job on a different estate; that is all the neighbours could tell Walter as he frantically knocked on every door to ask what had happened.

Walter was heartbroken, all he had left was the memory of Susan's sweet kiss and the last time he saw her walk away towards home with her lovely shiny hair reflecting the red of the evening sunset. That, and Susan accidentally, and loudly breaking wind as she walked away, looking back at him and blushing with embarrassment.

Sitting on the banks of Spigworth Pond in 1976, those feelings were still stirring inside him as he remembered Susan, it would be quite wrong for a grown man to feel that way about that little girl. However, for a short while, Walter had been 15 years old again, and for that, we should forgive him!

Perhaps it was best for Walter that he didn't know what had happened to Susan a little later on in life. Susan turned into a very naughty young woman who enticed any man she desired into her boudoir. One of her affairs was with the owner of the estate her father worked on. The owner Reginald Smearford, resided at Home Farm, it was a matter of moments before he fell for Susan in a big way.

Reginald, 35 years Susan's senior, had never experienced a physical side with a woman like her before. It was the most wonderful experience of his life. It was also the last experience of his life, Susan wore him so ragged that he suffered an enormous and fatal heart attack during their interlock of passion.

Unfortunately, for Susan, she had earned a reputation for herself, and a nickname, Suzie Seizure!

Just as Walter was surfacing from his daydream about Susan Caesar, a loud growl much like that from an angry dog erupted behind him. There was no need to fear, it was only Graham 'Gruffer' Wheeldon letting one of his signature tunes go!

Walter turned around sharply, after reality dawned on him as to who made the awful cacophony and stench, his eyes narrowed as he fought his urge to say, 'You really are a most unpleasant and disgusting swine!' Instead, he greeted Gruffer with a 'Happy New Year!'

"Allo Wiggy! Caught anything then?" asked Gruffer with a wince on his face as he forced another theme tune out.

"Yes I've caught a little jack pike and lost a nice roach to a gigantic pike." said Walter, still slightly annoyed.

"Not much doing then Wiggy." said Grufffer.

"No not a great deal, and incidentally my name is Walter, Walter Wigmore, not Wiggy. And if that is your way of being friendly my friend, then I must advise you that I do not appreciate it!" said Walter with an uncharacteristic bark.

"Sorry Walter, it's just that I have heard other club members refer to you as Wiggy and I thought that it was your nickname. Affectionate like, you know!" apologised Gruffer.

"Very well then Graham, as long as you now realise that is not the case." said Walter with a slight feeling of scoring a victory for the much maligned.

Walter also had feelings of bitterness beginning to rise inside him. Why should other anglers refer to him as 'Wiggy' other than abbreviating a surname? Did they think that he was bald underneath that Crabtree Trilby? In addition, if the nickname was used in jest or derision, then why?

Walter was quite aware that his angling prowess was not at the same level of success that other anglers attained. Yes, he would love to hold his head up with pride to say that he had regular success with his angling. Nevertheless, just because he wasn't able to, didn't mean that other anglers had the given right to deride him.

Walter believed that although skill and finesse were important in angling, a large spoonful of luck was always necessary to achieve success. Much like the chap on the pier who won the jackpot, he was in the right place at the right time, even if he did get a punch on the nose for it, he was still fortunate!

"Anyway Graham, have you come to fish today?" asked Walter.

"No mate, I just needed to get out of the house and get some fresh air." said Gruffer as he blew off once again.

It was probably the smelliest wafty whiffer that Gruffer had ever released into the wild, and its putrescence even stunned him.

"Anyway Wig…err Walter, must be off now, places to be, people to see matey. By the way, you've just missed three good bites while we were chatting!" said Gruffer.

Walter prayed for a South-West breeze to carry the shocking pong away, which never happened, God isn't that merciful!

Walter reeled his light float rig in to rid the hook of the little roach sucked, floppy and flaccid hollowed out skin where once a maggot resided, and replace it with a new maggot.

Walter stared at the bait box of slowly writhing maggots and drifted back off into another memory of his youth. He remembered one summer morning, walking to school with his friend Freddy Winter. Walking through the many dog mess infested twittens en route, they stumbled upon a blackbird lying beneath a hedgerow. Freddy pointed out that although some sort of scavenger had pecked the blackbird's eyes out, the little bird appeared to be alive and breathing.

Freddy picked the poor little blackbird up in his hands and said "Look Walter, its little chest is beating!"

Freddy gently stroked the breast of the little bird with his forefinger. Suddenly, the black feathers parted as the skin of the blackbird's breast split open to reveal a mass of squiggly white fly larvae. Dropping the obviously dead bird to the ground, Freddy's breakfast porridge saw the light of day once more as he heaved into a bush.

With Graham 'Gruffer' Wheeldon bidding a flatulent adieu, Walter was once again alone to enjoy the atmosphere of Spigworth Pond and its wildlife, in peace.

Peace, now that is a feeling that Walter had not experienced very often in his life. Walter was a caring individual who would often place others before him. That is a nice trait, but one can find oneself being taken advantage of, or for granted.

It was never more evident than in his late teens, that people took advantage of Walter's sweet nature. To be sociable and keep up the practice of human interactive skills, he would often find himself in situations where he would rather not have been. The Spinfield Boys Club held a charity dance to raise money for a rowing boat, which the Boys Club Leader William Screech thought would serve as an education in maritime for the boys.

It was the usual affair, warm orange squash and rich tea biscuits as refreshment, and a dance band made up from a small section of the Spinfield Municipal Orchestra conducted by the charismatic Jan Van Syke.

A 17 year old Walter, soon to become 18 years of age and ripe for National Service, went along to the dance with his old school mate Freddy and four girls, none of whom were known by Walter. Being a shy and gentle boy, Walter found it hard to relate to girls on any basis let alone one to one, conversations would often flicker out as quickly as they had ignited.

After Freddy had asked one of the girls to dance with him and two of the other girls were asked by some other boys for a dance, Walter was left alone with the remaining girl, Mildred Hargreaves. It was a very slow to begin with, but Mildred managed to coax a conversation out of Walter.

"What do you do in your spare time Walter?" asked Mildred.

"I like to go fishing whenever I can." Walter replied.

"Oh yes, what sea fishing?" Mildred asked with apparent interest.

"No, freshwater fishing!" said Walter proudly.

"Oh my dad goes sea fishing, out in a boat, deep sea fishing sometimes." said Mildred.

"Does he ever catch anything big?" asked Walter as he sat up straight with excitement.

"Oh yes, but mum doesn't like him bringing any of his fish home with him, well not since he brought a conger eel home last year anyway!" giggled Mildred.

"Was it very big?" asked Walter.

"Yes, I've got a photograph of it in my handbag if you'd like to see it." said Mildred, already fumbling about in the bottom of her handbag for her purse.

"Oh yes please Mildred?" pled Walter with the fervour of a deranged beagle.

"Look, that's my dad holding the great slippery thing in the kitchen." Mildred demonstrated by stroking her finger along the length of the conger eel, with naughty abandon.

"Cor, it's a big old eel isn't it!" said Walter.

"Yes it certainly is Walter!" laughed Mildred, putting her arm around Walter to give him a hug.

Walter could smell Mildred's clean and shampooed hair as her face neared his.

"Look, I'm bored Walter, will you walk me home please?" asked Mildred.

For this, Walter was grateful because he found it a reasonable excuse to get out of situation he didn't like to be in very much.

"I'd better tell Freddie that I'm going Mildred." said Walter.

"Okay, I'll be waiting here." said Mildred with a sultry sideways nod of her head.

Walter, reprieved from the dance, asked Mildred where she lived. It transpired that she lived just around the corner from his home.

It was a half hour walk home, but it was like climbing the very stairs to paradise for Walter. Mildred grabbed his hand and squeezed it tightly as she asked him if he had ever been out with a girl before. Walter told her of his brief romance with Susan Caesar at Deal Pond.

"Were you in love with her Walter?" asked Mildred with a smile.

"Well, I thought I was at the time, but looking back, I think it was more infatuation than anything, within a few weeks I'd grown used to the idea that she was no longer around." said Walter maturely.

As they neared her home, Mildred grabbed hold of Walter brutally and took him down a pathway that led to an allotment behind her home. Walter was giddy with part confusion and part excitement.

Mildred pushed Walter against a brick wall and forced herself upon him with a kiss as one he never knew could happen. She pressed her wonderful form against him and ruffled his hair with her hand.

Poor young Walter didn't really know what to do in this situation, apart from enjoy it of course, though he did find it a mite frightening and out of control.

By the time Mildred finished devouring him, Walter's hair was all sticky-up and brush-like at the back. His dishevelled mane would not seem out of place in this former part of the 21st Century, but in those days, decent folk would deem it as 'jolly untidy!'

From then on, it was the usual format, secret snogs and a little bit more on special occasions. Meeting the parents for Sunday tea and making a fool of one's self, fully believing that one had stuffed it up good and proper for the father ever to permit one proposing to his daughter; only to find the father welcoming you in on the next Sunday. Why are prospective father-in-laws so frightening?

Walter could not get Mildred out of his mind, she occupied his every thought and action, and he was truly in love.

Unbeknown to Walter, Mildred was a bit of a floozy on the quiet and was not faithful to him. This horrid fact dawned on him one heartbreaking evening out. It was Walter's 18th Birthday and some lads at The Spinfield Boys Club suggested they go for a real drink in the pub just up the road. The pub up the road, The Vineyard, was infamous for its clientele.

Walter was soon to be off for army conscription so he thought he would try a drop of beer to become more of a man. Unfortunately, for Walter, no matter how much of a man he felt he was, he did look rather young. He was refused service at the bar by the landlord, and walked out in humiliation as the other lads enjoyed their pints.

Walter walked back to the boys club to get his bicycle from the bike racks around the back of the premises. Unlocking his padlock, he heard a familiar sighing. It was Mildred cuddling the boys club leader's Teddy Boy son, Cliff Screech.

Anger, hatred and jealousy devoured Walter's very being as he lunged at Cliff with a viciousness he had never known before.

It was a fruitless gesture, Walter ended up with a bloody nose and wet trousers from falling into a filthy puddle. Just in case you weren't paying attention in Chapter 3, I thought I'd mention it once again.

Mildred found it funny and laughed like a crazed banshee. Walter failed to see the amusement and squelched his way home on his beloved bicycle, saddened, sodden and sobbing. The rotten cow!

Everything turned out okay for Walter eventually, with a lovely wife and two wonderful children. However, Walter would be a complete liar if he denied that Mildred was a higher education when it came to the physical side of things, he would also be a liar if he said that ever reached that height again!

Drifting back from his thoughts, Walter became aware of heavy footfalls and talking in the near vicinity, one of the voices he recognised was that of his son Stephen.

Walter turned around to see who was approaching, it was his son Stephen, his friend Ian Screech and his father, that... Teddy Boy, Cliff Screech!

"Hello Dad." said Stephen.

"Hello Stephen. What brings you here then?" asked Walter.

"Oh, Cliff and Ian took me to Padworth Park to try and catch some monster pike, but the park gate was closed because of bereavement in the park keeper's family, so we've come here to try our luck." explained Stephen.

"Hello Walter, long time, no see!" said Cliff.

"Err, hello Cliff, how are you?" asked Walter tentatively.

"Yes, not too bad thanks Walter, are you okay?" replied Cliff to return the concern as he took off his cap to scratch his head, revealing a bald and barren area that was once proudly crowned with a shining Brilliantine quiff.

"Well, all the best Walter, I'm going to find somewhere to fish, see you later." said Cliff.

Walter just nodded and gazed back at the water. Walter had only seen Cliff a small number of times, mostly in the precinct of Beaulieu Street in Spinfield Town Centre. Each time, Walter was quick enough to spot Cliff before Cliff saw him, and was able to duck into a shop to avoid him. There is something quite odd about a man who walks alone into a women's lingerie shop for no apparent reason; Walter wasn't aware of which shop he was in, he was only concerned with avoiding confrontation with Cliff.

It seemed like only half of an hour after setting up, that Stephen, Ian and Cliff Screech were doing battle with a pike or two; we all know how that feels when we've been struggling to catch and someone turns up and starts milking the pond of fish. There is almost something of a ring of a 'loaded one-arm bandit on the pier and watching some lucky git win everything' about it!

This vision of success unearthed a horribly bitter sensation in Walter's soul, the feeling of a score unsettled. Surely, Walter felt that he should have been over all that loathsome despising of Cliff Screech! Why, that was over twenty years ago! Why should it matter now? It is because a wrong will always be wrong, and the hurt the victim feels will always be there, one just learns to handle it better.

There was also the matter of seeing his son Stephen enjoying some jolly good fishing time with some pals. That was something that Walter was never able to give Stephen, as most, if not all of their adventures, were a complete and utter disaster.

So, it was envy then! Search deep into your heart and tell me you have never felt the caustic burn of envy, and I will call you a liar! Nevertheless, of all the company for his son to relish angling with, why did it have to be the Screech family?

Walter's float dipped as a fish took the maggot on the other end, and he missed it! Then another good bite and he missed that too!

Walter was all of a dither as he witnessed his offspring collaborating with the enemy.

It was late afternoon, and Walter grew tired of missing bites and seeing and hearing Stephen having a better time!

Cliff Screech got up out his chair and went for a wee in the bush at the back of his swim.

"Filthy beast, you wouldn't catch me doing that!" thought Walter with a full and bursting bladder after drinking too much coffee, and thinking that it might not be a bad idea if he relieved himself too.

On Walter's side of the pond, there were very few bushes to tinkle into, but there was one insignificant bush a few swims away from Walter's pitch. Around about waist height, the bush was just tall enough to hide Walter's shame; it took two good talks to himself before he braved the bush.

Walter performed the (for him) risky ritual, and the relief outweighed the timidity and reserve in him. Well, that was until he heard the cantering of horse hooves coming nearer.

It was a woman riding an impressive Thoroughbred Stallion.

Walter didn't know whether to hold on and wait for the female equestrian to pass, or carry on piddling. Even if he paused, the steam rising from his far warmer than air temperature tiddle would be a telltale sign. Walter chose to pause.

The woman on horseback looked at the secretly urinating Walter and halted her Stallion for a double take; she had recognized Walter!

"Walter, Walter! Is that you?" said the equestrian woman.

"Err, yes, 'tis me fine lady on horseback! Pray tell me, who are you?" requested Walter in his best medieval verbal finery of gentlemanliness.

"It's me, Susan, Susan Caesar. You must remember me surely?" asked Susan.

"Susan Caesar of The Deal?" asked Walter with eye rubbing disbelief.

"Yes it's me Susan you lovely man, I have often wondered if you still remembered me." said Susan with a tear in her eye.

"I have never forgotten you Susan, I will always remember those Saturdays at Deal Pond." Said Walter with a certain amount of strain; a man can only hold on for so long you know!

Susan told Walter that she was heartbroken when her father told her that they were relocating at a moment's notice, she didn't have the time to say goodbye to all her friends. Most of all, she regretted not exchanging addresses with Walter; at least she could have remained in contact.

"So how come you are back in this neck of the woods?" asked Walter.

"My grandmother passed away a few months ago at 102 years of age, and left her house in Spigworth village to me. I'm not sure if I want to live here again, my family live in Kingswood, near Grendon Underwood in Buckinghamshire, and we all rather like it there." explained Susan.

Susan went on to say that, she was mainly there to clear out and redecorate her grandmother's house, with the view of either selling or letting.

Before Walter had the chance to say that it was nice to see her again, another pheasant flew out from the rough, followed by a loud crack of a shotgun, sending the horse bolting, whisking Susan away into the distance.

Walter finished his pee in part ecstasy and part disappointment that Susan was once again, snatched from him, cruelly!

Walter sat down and reeled in his light float rig to remove yet another flaccid maggot skin from the hook, to replace it with a new one.

As sport slowed down, Cliff Screech thought he would go for a stroll and practice a bit of spinning with an artificial lure that was supposed to mimic an injured or dying perch. This meant he could move from swim to swim and find the pike, rather than wait for the pike to come to him. This also meant for Walter, dread upon dread, the likelihood of Cliff fishing near him, and a possible tense conversation of artificial humility would ensue as he passed him to spin in the next vacant swim.

What would Walter say to Cliff if he stopped to talk to him? It would definitely be small talk. Because in truth, they had never really been that close; not unless you count Cliff's fist punching Walter's face, which was the only real contact they had ever made.

With each unsuccessful plop of a spinner and whir of a fixed spool reel, swim by swim, Cliff came nearer to Walter's swim.

Eventually it had to happen, Cliff stopped by for a chat with a reluctant and uncharacteristically aloof Walter.

"Well Walter, incredibly long time, no see!" said Cliff loudly as he knelt down beside Walter.

"Not long enough!" thought Walter.

"Err yes Cliff, it has been a long time hasn't it." replied Walter half-heartedly.

"You've got a good son there Walter; he's a credit to you." Cliff assured Walter.

"Yes thank you Cliff, we have always tried to bring our boys up correctly." said Walter with a nod.

Cliff went on to say what a calming influence Stephen had been over Ian, and how much of a struggle it had been for he and his wife to steer their boys on a straight course. Unfortunately, their eldest son Robin was a lost cause it seemed. Robin became heavily involved with hard drugs and obviously, crime such as theft was his employment to finance his expensive habit.

"Oh dear, I'm very sad to hear that Cliff." said Walter with genuine sympathy.

"Yes, we thought we had paid enough attention to him as he grew up; but obviously the love and care we gave was not enough." said Cliff sadly.

"What do you think made him turn to drugs?" asked Walter.

"I don't know, but he did seem to change after his girlfriend and her family were killed in a car accident during Christmas 1973." replied Cliff.

"Does he live with you?" asked Walter.

"No, we had to throw him out because he was stealing and selling stuff from home. He emptied Ian's Post Office Savings account that we had started for him when he was born." replied Cliff with his eyes welling up with tears.

"Well I don't think you should hold yourselves responsible for the way he has turned out Cliff, when a child is born there is no telling which path they may take as they mature." said Walter with sympathy.

"Well, I just feel that we must have done something wrong, I mean, even Ian has had a brush with the law." said Cliff.

"Oh dear, nothing serious I hope?" Walter asked.

"No, stealing from fishing tackle Woolworths and music cassettes from W H Smith, but it still isn't good." Cliff replied with a frown.

Cliff went on to say that ever since Ian had been pals with Stephen, he had become a very good boy. Walter was proud and pleased to hear that.

"Hey, do you remember Mildred Hargreaves Walter?" asked Cliff with desire to change the topic of conversation.

"Err, yes I do Cliff, as far as I remember she was my girlfriend until I saw you with her behind the boy's club!" said Walter sternly.

"Oh crumbs, yes! I punched you on the bugle didn't I." remembered Cliff.

Then Cliff went on to tell him that he thought Mildred was his girlfriend too, but that it turned out she was seeing plenty of other boys as well.

"I'm sorry I hit you Walter, the truth is that you startled me in the darkness and I lashed out, I didn't even know it was you." explained Cliff with genuine remorse.

"What happened to Mildred?" enquired Walter.

"Oddly enough, I heard that she became a Nun and later became a missionary!" Cliff replied with a bit of a giggle in his voice.

Walter exploded into laughter. After the hysterics subsided and the burning tears of laughter were wiped away, Walter said that he couldn't imagine anyone less likely to become a Nun.

"As far as I can remember Mildred wasn't even Catholic, and imagining her submitting herself to the ties of chastity seems even more absurd!" chortled Walter.

"Ha ha yes, she must have really had a calling!" said Cliff, joining in on the hilarity.

After a little more conversation, Cliff noticed that Walter's bung float had submerged and disappeared.

"I think you've got a pike on Walter." said Cliff, pointing in the direction of the recently vanished float.

"Wha... Crikey, thanks Cliff!" shouted Walter with excitement.

This was perhaps, time to redeem the big pike Walter hooked and lost during Antique Bluey's charity match in October.

The battle between Esox and Walter raged for a long time, seemingly forever. Line stripped from the reel spool with aggression as the pike made several desperate bids for freedom.

In the end, as all good fishing stories go, the pike eventually tired, and Cliff Screech performed the honour of netting the fish.

15lbs 12oz was the weight of Walter's pike. Walter was more than happy!

Cliff called his son Ian to bring the camera to take a photograph of Walter, his prize pike and he!

Two cheesy smiles, and a click from a Polaroid Instant Camera with possible blurry consequences, Walter returned his pike to Spigworth Pond.

A bond was made between Walter and Cliff that day, they grew to like each other and fished together occasionally for many years to come.

All the years of unwarranted animosity dissolved. Okay, one can never get those wasted years back, but one can try their level best to erase the past and make good of the present. There were too many years of unrequited friendship, and all because of a silly girl!

*Little did Walter know he was chomping on one of the last bars of Five Boys; in 1976, Fry's withdrew the quaint little chocolate bar from sale.

CHAPTER 10

VALENTINE'S DAY AND A LILAC DRESS

February was cold with wet snow, and the fishing on Spigworth Pond was unremarkable. However, when the fishing is poor and the cold and boredom starts to set in, anglers get up for a walk and possibly chat to each other. Conversations will range from how poor the fishing is, to football and possibly television.

On Saturday, February 7th 1976, the hot topic of gossip on the banks of Spigworth Pond was Head Bailiff, Mark Gosling and a mystery woman.

It was common knowledge that Mark Gosling wasn't much of a hit with the girls, his usual expressions of one who is about to punch you and a bulldog chewing a scorpion probably didn't help him very much.

Nevertheless, Mark had been seen in the Fine Fare supermarket with an attractive woman on his arm and a shopping basket on the other.

Who was the mystery woman they all wondered? More importantly, how did an ugly git like Mark Gosling ever end up with a cracker like that?

The mystery woman in question was Christine Blanchette, a 38-year-old widow who had employed Mark's skills as a gardener on the basis that she had heard from a neighbour that he was handy with a spade and fork.

Mark first met Christine on a November Saturday afternoon when she needed her garden clearing of nettles, brambles and a general jungle of dying and overgrown foliage.

The pair forged a sort of friendship when Mark had cut and scratched his face badly on a vicious tentacle of blackberry thorns. Christine cleansed and nursed his wounds in the kitchen, and then gave him a cup of tea and some digestive biscuits.

Christine was lonely and needed to talk with somebody, she told Mark of her late husband and showed him a photograph album of happier times.

Christine's husband John was a Metropolitan Policeman, tragically killed two years before in a bungled bank robbery. The young bank robber hadn't intended to kill John, the shotgun went off accidently after it was thrown down on the floor when the offender panicked and attempted to make a run for freedom.

Christine sobbed heavily as she told Mark of her great love for John, she thought that she had come to terms with her grief, but it had been a long time since she last spoke to anyone about him.

Mark was filled with genuine sadness for her and offered her a grubby handkerchief to dry her tears. Christine's tears subsided and she thanked Mark for being so thoughtful and being a good listener.

"Anyway, I think your wife must be expecting you home soon, the light is fading fast and you won't be able to do any more work in the garden today." said Christine as she took two pound notes from her purse as payment for Mark's work.

"Err, no you're alright, you pay me when I've finished the job, I'll be back tomorrow morning to finish off." said Mark as he put on his jacket and cap to leave.

"That's very kind of you! Are you sure your wife won't mind?" asked Christine.

"No she won't mind, on the account that I am a bachelor." answered Mark with a rare smile.

"Oh, then would you like to stay for Sunday lunch then?" offered Christine.

"That would be nice, yes, thank you!" said Mark with gratitude.

At 8:00 the following morning, Mark arrived at Christine's house in his van with his gardening tools.

After a lingering ring of the front door bell, Christine opened the door, an aromatic mix of expensive perfume and sizzling bacon wafted out, tantalising Mark's nostrils.

"I'm just cooking a full English breakfast; there are plenty of sausages, bacon rashers, eggs and mushrooms. Would you like to join me?" asked Christine with the certainty of Mark accepting.

Mark had only eaten a bowl of cornflakes that morning, so there was plenty of room for a spot of fry up.

"Yes, that would be nice, thank you." replied Mark quickly, as though the special offer was just about to expire.

The breakfast table conversation drifted from a debate to whether Daddy's Sauce was better than OK Sauce, onto 'they don't make eggs like they used to' and eventually 'Fairy Liquid is superior to any other brand of washing-up liquid!' 'You wash, and I'll wipe!"

After the hearty breakfast and a certain amount of appreciative belching, Mark got down to business with the mess that was once a beautiful garden.

By 11:00am, Mark had virtually cleared the garden and was soon carrying out old coal sacks filled with chopped up weeds, bramble and branches to his van. Mark would take the sacks to the Spinfield Community tip the following weekend. If you've ever left a sack of rotting weeds in the back of your car, you will appreciate the nasty niff that permeated Mark's van for quite some time after.

Christine asked Mark if he'd like to scrub up in the shower before dinner, there were clean towels on the heated towel rail. Mark declined the offer and settled for washing his hands instead, it was far too early to strip off in a lady's house, even if it was in a hygienic capacity.

At 12:30pm, at the dong of a dinner gong, a wonderful roast dinner was steaming away on the table. Considerate Christine brought the vegetables to the table in heated bowls separately. There is always embarrassment when someone assumes one likes all the vegetables and one leaves a portion of offending veg on the plate with knife and fork side by side, parallel and central in the 'I've finished!' presentation.

"Oh don't you like sprouts?"

"No, not really."

"They are very good for you!"

In addition, the long irritating argument that may ensue "Well, of all the rudeness, I've prepared and cooked a lovely meal, and all you do to show your thanks is to waste some of it! There are children starving in poorer countries, you should be ashamed of yourself..." and so on.

Fortunately, for Christine, Mark loved all vegetables and the only problem she had was making sure he had left enough for her to eat.

"There's a raspberry trifle for afters if you like Mr Gosling." said Christine.

"Cor, smashing!" was Mark's reply.

After a number of weeks and Sunday dinners, a romance blossomed. Mark appeared to be taking things slowly, but truth to tell, with his lack of experience he wasn't sure how fast to go!

Christine liked the fact that Mark was a bit slow on the uptake; it was a refreshing change to meet a man who enjoyed her company and who was in no rush to consummate their relationship.

The thoughts of fishing Spigworth Pond were never far from Mark's mind, but those thoughts didn't occupy his mind as much as those of Christine.

How could he be so lucky? He was a man in his mid fifties and Christine was only 38 years of age. What did she see in him? She was beautiful, he was overweight, red faced, and didn't feel that he was particularly handsome. What would he do if it all went wrong? What Mark didn't realise, was that Christine had fallen for his kindness, he was also doing something else regularly and unwittingly, smiling.

Mark began to spend more and more time with Christine, but he did miss his fishing. Eventually he was going to have to ask Christine if she would like to accompany him on a fishing trip one day, but he was afraid to in case she declined.

Nevertheless, one weekend Christine surprised Mark when she asked him what he would have normally done in his free time before he had met her.

Mark gingerly told her that he liked to fish.

"Oh great! What, freshwater fishing?" asked Christine with apparent delight.

Mark told her of his favourite place, Spigworth Pond. It transpired that her deceased husband was an avid angler, and that they had both spent a lot of time on the banks of rivers and ponds. This was impossible, this could not be happening. Mark was waiting to wake up with disappointment from a wonderful dream.

How could a man have so much luck? Christine was the most beautiful woman he had ever known, and not just beautiful in appearance. She was an excellent cook, and wonder of wonders, she liked fishing!

It wasn't long before the first fishing trip was arranged. Christine wasn't able to fish Spigworth Pond because she wasn't a member of Mark's club, but she knew of a lovely day ticket water 10 miles north in a village called Middlewind. The day ticket water was a 2-mile stretch of a lovely little river called The Wither. The lovebirds were soon making plans to go fishing together.

Mark and Christine made their way to Middlewind one frosty and early December Saturday morning in Mark's van, full of expectation and romance. After driving over the bridge that crossed The Wither, they arrived in Middlewind. Christine directed Mark to park his van outside the village store, Middlewind Mart where they purchased day tickets, and for Christine, a 14-day rod licence from the post office section in the corner of the little shop.

Christine had prepared a picnic for them to eat at lunchtime. It was simple fare, a flask of oxtail soup, a flask of hot chocolate, egg sandwiches, cheese and pickle sandwiches, sausage rolls, scotch eggs, pork pies, crisps and chocolate digestives. Simple fare if you are used to taking all that lot fishing with you that is! Mark wasn't used to that kind of nosh, and his eyes nearly popped out of their sockets when Christine opened the hamper to show him what he had to look forward to.

The piscatorial lovebirds took their fishing tackle out of the van and made their way to the bridge to look at the river. Mark thought the river was beautiful and immediately fell in love with it. Swift shallow clear water, with streaming water crowfoot swaying in the current was not familiar to Mark. The little river fishing he had done had been on deep, dirty brown tidal rivers that looked most unattractive. In the spring and early summer, the water crowfoot revealed its true beauty, adorned with little yellow and white flowers.

Christine knew of a good place to start fishing, a place that she and her late husband fished many times with fair success.

They walked about 400 yards upstream, until a bend in the river, lined with overhanging bushes and small trees came into view. There was also a very comfortable pitch for two anglers to nestle in close to water level; this always makes the landing and returning of fish easier.

After fishing for a few hours, Mark was more relaxed than he had ever been before. Mark always used to detest people speaking to him when he was fishing, but he enjoyed talking to Christine so much that he missed a few good bites.

Before he knew it, it was picnic time with all that lovely grub. After drinking a few cups of hot chocolate and a cup of soup, Mark was concerned that he may have to blow his courteous cover and go for a wee. A little while later, Christine emerged from a bush after relieving herself, so he needn't have worried.

The fishing that day wasn't much to talk about, but the time passed too quickly for Mark. As they made their way back to the car, Christine suggested that they buy some crusty white bread and locally made mature cheddar from the village shop, cheese on toast was on the cards. Christine also bought a nice bottle of French red wine to drink with the cheesy treat.

"I'm afraid I won't be able to drink any of the wine Christine, I won't be able to drive home." said Mark with concern.

"Who said you have to go home?" said Christine.

"Um, I haven't brought my pyjamas with me!" Mark responded in panic.

"Don't be silly, you don't need pyjamas, the bedroom is lovely and warm." Christine assured Mark.

This was a difficult situation for Mark, apart from a little bit of titillation with a girl at a party in his youth, he had never been fortunate enough to spend the night with a woman.

Christine ensured Mark that she was well aware how difficult this would be for him, but she would be kind to him so that he didn't feel awkward or nervous. Nevertheless, Mark did feel incredibly uncomfortable and it would have been the easiest thing in the world to just drive Christine home and leave her. However, the thought of spoiling something special that may never come again, gave him the Great British stiff upper lip to soldier on and stay.

The following morning at breakfast, Mark wore a grin so broad; it was as though someone had put a coat hanger in his mouth overnight. Christine also looked quite pleased with herself.

The romance blossomed, and Mark invited Christine to the Spinfield Coarse Angling Club's Valentine's Day dance held at Spinfield Assembly Hall, led by the Sheila Tilcroft Show Band. Very conveniently, Valentine's Day fell on a Saturday. The dance was a fund raising event, with the target to raise enough money in the kitty to buy a new boathouse and a petrol powered grass trimmer for the close season work parties. There were bumper raffle prizes comprising of a romantic weekend break for two in Paris (that's an obvious description, it would hardly be a romantic weekend break in Paris for one, three perhaps but not one!), a magnum of Moët et Chandon Champagne and a bumper box of Terry's All Gold chocolates. However, there was an additional prize for the best dancing couple, a pair of S.C.A.C. club permits for the 1976-1977 season.

Dancing wasn't actually Mark's cup of tea, he had to wrestle with his selfish side to pluck up the courage to buy a pair of tickets. Nevertheless, when one is in love, one finds oneself doing allsorts to show one's devotion for the other. Doesn't one?

At 7:00pm on the evening of February 14th 1976, there was a dreadful noise of chatter and laughter from the gaggle of dancers at the Spinfield Assembly Hall. Loud voices of the already tipsy anglers shouting out insults to each other:-

"Oi Fred! I don't fancy yours much!"
"Neither do I Jim, she's your wife not mine ho ho!"

And:-
"Does your wife know that you're out? He he!"
"Yeah! Your wife obviously doesn't Hoo Hoo!"
And so on, such jolly japes!

At 7:30pm, Mark and Christine walked into the hall, arm in arm. The gaggle and giggling stopped as each dancer stared open mouthed at the loving couple. There was no doubt about it, Christine looked absolutely stunning, and the other women present confirmed that with catty criticism. There was even more amazement at how smart and handsome Mark looked, it took a moment for the penny to drop to the angling club members as to who it was. The transformation from combat jacket to Tuxedo was not something Mark was comfortable with; but after a few nice compliments, he began to feel good about himself. Mark went to the bar to get some drinks and overheard the conversations of other anglers, boring the Y-Fronts off each other as they boasted about their personal bests and expertise.

Most of the Spigworth regulars were there, Gruffer Wheeldon, full of wind and corking it up to be polite so as not to offend his wife, Walter Wigmore on his own with a fizzy cola, Badger Bill Parsons with his girlfriend and Peter Burt eyeing up the talent, to name just a few.

Three completely unrecognisable anglers that turned out to be Jed Cleminson, Will Spring and Rick Western the carp anglers minus the makeup and drag, took their wives along for a bit of a boogie.

Little Peter Burt the Squirt, ever hopeful that he may find a girl that night, was chased about the hall all evening by a very tall and plump girl. The girl in question, Janice Pragnell, was desperate for a man, and Squirt was going to be the one!

Despite Squirt's obvious protests of 'Leave off!', 'Get off!', 'Go away please?' comments, he and Janice disappeared for an hour and a half during the evening. Janice returned to the dance with her dress inside out, Squirt had a nasty bruise like mark on his neck, and a silly grin on his face!

Walter Wigmore had absolutely no idea why he was there, other than his love and support for the S.C.A.C.

At one point in the evening the guests, celebrity dance troop, Fred Fawcett and his Tap Dancing Troupe Supreme, danced to Putting on the Ritz, sung by Sheila Tilcroft and her band.

As a clever twist to their dance routine, the girls in Fred's troupe dressed as Ritz cracker biscuit boxes. This pitiful, painful and embarrassing performance earned rowdy applause, not because anyone enjoyed it, but because the spectacle was finally over.

Spinfield Assembly Hall sued Fred Fawcett and his Tap Dancing Troupe Supreme a few days later for scratching the dance floor with their tap shoes. This was regardless of the fact that the floor suffered damage from cigarette and spliff burns from Hawkwind fans at a recent concert. It was quite simple really; the chairman of Spinfield Assembly Hall loved Hawkwind and loathed tap dancing!

Everyone who was eager to win the double season ticket prize went on to the dance floor to sweat it out to do their very best in convincing the judges that they could dance. Half way through the competition, the dancers separated into a circle, leaving Graham Gruffer Wheeldon and his wife dancing alone in the centre. This ritual, normally reserved for the happy newlywed couple to lead the dance, was in this instance because Gruffer finally lost control of his flatulence and people ran to get away from the stench.

This worked to an advantage for Gruffer and his wife, the spotlight fell on the couple and they won the double season ticket prize. Was there no end to this flatulent angler's luck?

Squirt disappeared with Janice Pragnell once again, and returned looking like the Joker in Batman with badly applied lipstick.

Walter Wigmore was on his second bottle of cola, and still wondering why he was at the dance. Unexpectedly, Walter felt a hand slip into his, with a soft voice "Shall we dance?"

"You don't remember me do you Walter?" asked the soft voice.

It was Mildred Hargreaves, alive, well and living in the town of Spinfield.

"Mildred"? Walter asked in puzzlement.

"Oh you do remember me, you dear, dear man!" said Mildred excitedly.

"Oh yes, I do remember you Mildred. I was talking about you with one of your old acquaintances not so long ago." said Walter.

"Ha ha! You mean Cliff Screech don't you!" laughed Mildred.

"Yes, and I believe he is here tonight." said Walter.

"Ooh yes, I know, I've already seen him! It was a bit of a shock to see him actually." said Mildred.

Mildred then went on to say that the last time she spoke to Cliff, he was a Teddy Boy with a huge greasy quiff.

"And now he looks as though he has been cruelly scalped by a vicious tribe of Red Indians!" Mildred chuckled sinisterly.

"Apache?" asked Walter.

"Yes, a little bit patchy, but in general most men go bald symmetrically." said Mildred.

Walter burst into hysterical laughter "No, APACHE, Apache Indians!"

"Oh I'm sorry, the music is quite loud and I don't hear that well these days." Mildred apologized.

"No, no need to apologize Mildred. That is one of the fondest memories I have of you, you made me laugh a lot." Walter said with a kind smile.

"I also hurt you Walter, I remember that and I am very sorry." said Mildred with genuine remorse.

"That's okay, all part of growing up I suppose." said Walter with acceptance.

Walter asked Mildred what she was doing there at the dance and that he had no idea she had any connection with the angling club. Mildred told him that her next-door neighbour, an elderly man who was a member of the club, invited her.

"Oh, and your husband doesn't mind?" asked Walter.

"I never married Walter, as you probably know I became a nun." said Mildred.

"But you're not a nun anymore?" asked Walter.

"Well, nuns don't make a habit of dressing up in low cut ball gowns as a rule." Mildred said with a smile.

"Ha ha ha ha ha! Very good, HABIT! Ha ha ha ha!" laughed Walter with great guffaw.

"He he he he! Yes, it was good wasn't it!" said Mildred, pretending she meant it to be a joke.

Mildred explained that due to grave reasons of misbehaviour, she was an exclaustrated nun, no longer allowed to wear the habit. She wasn't allowed to marry in the Catholic church either.

Mildred was pleased to hear that Walter was happily married and had a lovely little family.

"You deserve to be happy Walter, you are one of the loveliest men I have ever known." said Mildred with tears welling in her eyes as she parted to join her dance partner.

The memory of romance between Walter and Mildred was merely the aroma of some once beautiful, dead flowers in a vase.

However, in full blossom, the romance between Mark and Christine was clear for all to see, they could not keep away from each other.

The end of evening drew close, and it was time to draw the raffle tickets.

Mark had bought a couple of raffle tickets without Christine knowing.

Singer, Sheila Tilcroft announced that the guest celebrity dancer Fred Fawcett would be drawing the raffle, to boos, jeers and flying saucers of paper plates.

"Now then, now then! Behave please ladies and gentlemen?" said Sheila Tilcroft in protest.

Fred Fawcett was enraged and very hurt by the crowd's response, he refused to draw the tickets and fled in a flap of top hat and tails, repressed tears and vowing to never perform in Spinfield ever again!

Sheila Tilcroft took on the responsibility of the raffle draw. Digging deep with her hand to the bottom of the box of tickets, Sheila pulled out a ham and mustard sandwich that must have found its way in there when all the paper plate throwing was going on. Sheila made a second attempt and pulled out pink ticket number 32.

"The first ticket drawn is…pink 32!" said Sheila proudly.

"What's the prize?" someone shouted out in the dim light.

"The prize for pink ticket number 32 is…a bulk spool of 5lbs breaking strain monofilament line donated by F.W. Woolworth of Spinfield!" Sheila said excitedly without a single clue of what she had just been talking about.

"I ain't got it then!" shouted out the same voice with disagreeable disgust.

"Um, pink ticket 32 anyone?" asked Sheila.

Apparently, no one would own up to buying pink ticket 32, the prize was too much of a disappointment!

Sheila dug her hand deep into the box again to pull out another ticket.

"Blue ticket number 101?" Sheila begged for some sort of response.

No one responded.

"Blue ticket 101, the prize is a magnum of champagne!!!!!" said Sheila in earnest.

"I've got it, I've got it!" said Peter 'Squirt' Burt excitedly.

"Well done!" said Sheila with relief.

Sheila then whispered "You can have the box of chocolates as well, I'm having a hard time here!"

Peter went back to his new girlfriend Janice Pragnell.

"Here you are Janice, we'll enjoy this lot tomorrow if you like." said Squirt.

Janice had every intention to make 'tomorrow' happen and enjoying that lot, she was in love!

After a few more crumby prizes such as a box of Newberry Fruits and a packet of Mustad O'

Shaughnessy hooks, Sheila pulled out the bumper prize ticket

"And now, the very last prize, and a very special one…yellow ticket 97 for the romantic weekend break in Paris for two!"

Mark Gosling fumbled around in his jacket pockets for the tickets; he remembered one of the tickets he bought was number 97, but couldn't remember what colour it was. He couldn't find the tickets.

Christine looked down at the floor and saw a yellow ticket.

"There's a ticket on the floor near your foot Mark. Is it yours?" Christine asked Mark.

Mark picked ticket the up, it was yellow 97.

"Yep, I've got it!" Mark shouted.

"Well done!" Sheila congratulated Mark.

Mark and Christine felt on top of the world that night. Mark couldn't believe his luck and how his world had changed for the better.

The following morning at breakfast, Christine asked Mark if he would go shopping in Spinfield town the following weekend. Mark said he would love to, as long as they could eat out!

The following weekend came and Mark and Christine walked around the shops of Spinfield. They mostly visited the shops that Christine wanted to go into.

They visited a women's clothes store and Christine saw a lilac dress she fell in love with, but with a price tag of £30 it was more than she could afford. Mark kept that in mind, as he had wanted to buy Christine a present.

They then visited a jeweller and looked at rings. (You can see where this is going can't you!)

"Do you know that it's leap year this year Mark?" said Christine.

"Yes I do." said Mark.

"A woman is allowed to propose marriage to the man of her heart's desire on a leap year!" said Christine with a smile.

"I didn't know that." said Mark with puzzled wonderment.

"Yes, so you see that engagement ring in the middle at the top in the presentation case?" asked Christine.

"Yes." said Mark.

"My ring size is K! Will you marry me please Mark?" Christine proposed.

Mark was very flustered and didn't know quite what to say.

Christine told Mark that she wouldn't push him into anything and that she would like him to think about it.

"I will propose to you again on Leap Day, if you don't wish to marry me, tradition has it that you must buy me twelve pairs of gloves, but I have no use for gloves, the lilac dress will do." said Christine.

Mark's life had completely changed, and he knew that Christine was the chief reason for that. However, marriage would be such a deep dive into responsibility and he wasn't certain how he felt about it. He spent the whole week thinking of nothing else, he had to make his mind up. If he chose not to marry Christine, would she still want him? Mark definitely wanted to keep seeing her, and he knew deep down that he was in love with her. What was he to do?

A complete week had passed, and the morning of Sunday 29th February 1976 found Mark arriving at

Christine's home with his decision, and a large box under his arm. Mark rang the doorbell.

"Oh, come in Mark?" asked Christine nervously.

Mark's facial expression was that of an angling club Head Bailiff.

"Well, have you made up your mind yet?" asked Christine.

"Yes, I have." said Mark handing the large box to Christine.

Christine took the box and opened it; it was the lilac dress.

"Oh, it's the dress!" said Christine with a tinge of disappointment in her voice.

Christine took the dress out of the box and pulled it up against her body.

"How does it look?" asked Christine.

"It looks lovely, it would look lovelier with the other thing that's in the bottom of the box." said Mark nodding at the box.

In the bottom of the box, was a small, velvet covered heart shaped box.

Christine took the little box, with shaking hands, she opened it; inside was the engagement ring.

"Oh Mark, I do love you!" Christine cried as she threw her arms around him.

"Well, I thought I may as well get you a dress to wear at the registry office when we get married!" Mark said with a gentle smile. The big softy!

CHAPTER 11

THE IDES OF MARCH

Monday 1st March 1976, the dawn of the third month of the year starts a pendulum swinging like the sword of Damocles over the coarse angler's head.

After fourteen days have passed, the coarse angler will face three months of abstinence from his or her favourite pastime. For March 15th, the Ides of March in the Roman calendar and the anniversary of the assassination of Julius Caesar is also the beginning of the coarse fishing close season.

At the end of the coarse fishing season, an angler can reflect on successes and failures of the past season, where it all went wrong and when it all went right. Maybe the next season will all go right for some!

For three months in the 1976 close season, some anglers nagged by their spouses to do the jobs that they were supposed to do last close season, would attempt to do at least part of their chores. Some anglers would strip down their old split cane rods, re-whip, re-varnish them, check the rod rings for wear, clean and lubricate their reels. Some anglers with the modern fibreglass rods of the day would just check the whippings and rod rings for wear. The lazy anglers that didn't check those simple things would wonder why they lost fish as their line frayed during the following season as a result.

The fortunate anglers living near the coast would try their hands at sea fishing. They eagerly decipher the tide timetables to decide when to get a backache from digging lugworm for bait. The lazy gits with more money than sense bought their lugworms from a fishing tackle shop, wrapped in yesterday's newspaper.

It may not be so easy to accustom oneself to the concept of using such heavy tackle in ratio to the size of the fish caught. Fourteen pounds breaking strain line, four-ounce lead weights, a dirty great hook for a twelve ounce flounder would seem a bit weird to the angler who has been used to playing and landing a four pound tench on two pounds breaking strain line and size 16 hook.

The angler with money who preferred to be beside a river, lake or pond with light tackle, would possibly have a bash at fly-fishing for trout, snagging trees and bank side flora around them with the uncontrollable length of line necessary to cast a fly to a rising rainbow or brown trout. Fly casting takes time to practice. Once perfected, or at least to the best of the angler's ability, the finesse of a fly line gently settling on the surface of the water is a sight for sore eyes. The straightening and tightening of that line as a trout takes the fly is a sight even more satisfying!

All of these things, they would do to ease the pain of separation from the coarse anglers' raison d'être.

There were of course close season work parties, where all members of the angling club were obliged to attend as a condition of club membership. It is funny how a club that contained over 100 members would only ever see a fifth of those attending the work parties, and the same faces attending every year.

Now in the 21st Century of course, the close season for coarse fishing doesn't necessarily apply to landlocked still waters, just the watercourses that flow to end eventually at the ocean, or if a private fishing club says so. There is no doubt that despite whether it is or is not ethical to fish for coarse fish on still waters year in, year out, the banks look so much better for not being trampled on by wellington boots and fishing trolleys for three months.

Back in 1976 at Spigworth Pond however, the impending sentence of piscatorial refrain loomed for the club members of the Spinfield Coarse Angling Club.

It was time to pack in as much fishing time as possible before the death knell of March 15th; and good old Walter Wigmore was not going to miss out.

Walter's season was poor in comparison to other anglers' standards, but considering Walter's reputation for not catching fish very often, he was relatively pleased with his results. He had though, unwittingly upgraded from a Mr Crabtree clown to an angler who caught a few fish, even if by fluke rather than skill.

Walter booked a one-week holiday off work so that he could fish the last week of the season. The original plan was that Walter and his newfound chum Squirt, would fish together that week. Sadly, for Walter though, since Squirt's encounter with Janice Pragnell at the angling club's charity dance, he hadn't been fishing at all, he chose to cancel his week with Walter, he was way too much in love!

No matter, Walter enjoyed his fishing, and even on his own, with so much wildlife around him, he was never truly alone.

Walter decided to adopt the pike and tiddler approach again for his week holiday, one rod out for pike, and one to catch roach and whatnot to keep him busy.

The weather forecast for the week was for settled conditions, dry and sunny by day, with threats of subzero pond-freezing temperatures during the night.

Spigworth pond was abundant with wildfowl, which often kept the water moving during the night as they desperately searched for food to keep warm, and alive.

Nonetheless, on Monday March 8th 1976, Walter was not impressed to see a pair of swans standing on a platform of ice, looking confused as to why their usual medium of transport had solidified.

Walter scanned the water with his binoculars and observed frenzied and maniacal coots chasing each other about at the north end of the pond in a small section that was ice-free. It was worth trying.

Arriving at the north end of the pond it appeared that only peg 13 was fishable. Spigworth Pond was one of the few local fisheries where you would find a peg 13. A few local angling clubs didn't have a thirteenth swim on their fisheries. For match fishing in particular, to draw peg 13 would kick the confidence out of any superstitious angler. The S.C.A.C. chose to keep continuity of numbers because even if peg 13 was called 12B or 14, it would still be the thirteenth swim, and in the end, it is unlikely that fish can count and will pick up a bait from anywhere if they are hungry.

Some believe that the origin of unlucky number 13 stemmed from The Last Supper. Judas Iscariot, the man who betrayed Christ, took thirteenth place at the table. The reality is of course is that if there were fourteen at the table and Judas was the fourteenth, fourteen would have been an unlucky number.

The baker's dozen is thirteen, which came about because one could never guarantee the weight of loaves, so the baker would add an extra loaf to the dozen as a makeweight.

In some parts of the world, a baker who diddled a customer out of bread was likely to receive a fine or severe punishment. In Egypt, a baker who ripped a customer off would have his ear nailed to the bakery door. In Babylon, the baker would have a hand cut off. A very good reason to shove another loaf in then!

It is possible that the thirteenth loaf represented the loaf Judas had in front of him on the table at The Last Supper. Is number thirteen unlucky? You get thirteen loaves and only pay for twelve. How unlucky is that?

Walter wasn't superstitious anyway, his favourite pastime was chequered with disaster, so the number 13 was irrelevant. There was ice in the margins and to ensure a safe return of fish, Walter proceeded to break the ice with his landing net pole; the ice was quite thin and easy to crack.

The early morning Sun rose above the trees and highlighted the vapour of Walter's breath as he exhaled, it felt good to be alive. With a bit of luck, the Sun would help to thaw a bit more of the pond, the over excited coots would do the rest.

There is a great feeling of achievement in catching a fish on a heavily frozen pond, especially when other anglers can't be bothered to try their luck.

On the roadside bank, the pair of swans decided to go for a bit of a skate on the ice. There was a loud crack and panic of large white wings as one of the swans found a thin patch in the ice. The commotion and movement of water underneath made the icy covering tinkle and crackle audibly throughout its entirety as the frozen canopy flexed and rocked on the surface of the pond.

The swan was having difficulty getting back up onto the ice, and the hole that it made falling through gradually became larger. The struggling swan's fellow mate panicked and fled to the roadside bank. Eventually though, with all the flapping about, the ice imprisoned swan managed to get to safety, not of course that it was ever in danger!

Because of the ice, there wasn't enough room in peg 13 to fish two rods comfortably, so Walter settled on the maggot and float approach, at least for the time being until more open water became available if the thaw progressed sufficiently.

Walter fed a few maggots into the swim to tempt a roach or two to feed. It was one of those wonderful mornings with no breeze to hamper the cast of light float tackle. All Walter needed was to get a bite; the tiniest roach would suffice on a cold morning such as that.

The morning passed slowly without event, but the ice had thawed sufficiently for Walter to cast out a sprat on his pike rod. It was time for Walter to load his pipe for a smoke, and a bit of a daydream.

He thought about the ensuing close season and how he would occupy his time. The close season would be a good time to iron out the wrinkles of the previous season. He wondered whether his son James would want to go fishing with him in the new season, or whether the Mr Crabtree Trilby would hang on the eternal hat stand, with no Peter to save the day.

He thought about the previous year, it wasn't all disaster. Considering he had earned a reputation of being an angler who couldn't catch a single fish, he did have some memorable, even if accidental moments. There was the big tench that he had caught and netted, only to watch it swim away from the landing net he had kept it in so that he could show his son James when he had returned from the village shop with the fizzy and crisp supplies. Only Walter knew how big that tench was, and he could still feel the bitter disappointment eight months on.

There was the big perch, admittedly caught by mistake during Antique Bluey's memorial pike match; the perch didn't count, but a lot of anglers would kill to catch a fish as marvellous as that! The massive pike he almost landed in the same match, only to be lost because of a light hook hold, and that farting monster Gruffer Wheeldon making Peter 'Squirt' Burt falter as he attempted to land the fish for him, knocking the hook out of the pike with the landing net. Yes, in retrospect, Walter had done extremely well!

There was still nothing happening, still no bobs on the float, so Walter carried on daydreaming. He thought about the angling days of his youth, it seemed as though he had more luck as an angler when he was a boy, nearly always catching something, if only tiddlers. However, the ponds he fished were small, heavily stocked and hungry. In comparison, Spigworth was massive with plenty of places for fish to feed at will. To have the same success as Walter did on Deal Pond for instance, Spigworth would have to be ridiculously overstocked, the fish sizes would be pathetic and so not much point in fishing it.

Walter thought about his lovely old dad, he wasn't ever really that interested in fishing, but he enthused because of the love of his son. It all seemed a bit topsy-turvy to Walter, he had two sons, possibly due to embarrassment Steven would rather go fishing without his father, and James wasn't really that interested in fishing anyway. A father possesses a rare prize when he has a child that is as equally enthusiastic about the same pastime.

Walter's father to tell the truth was never a patient man and so was not ever going to make an angler; he nonetheless took Walter fishing many times.

Walter remembered that flies and wasps seemed to be attracted to his dad. Mr Wigmore used Brilliantine on his hair; this seemed to draw flying insects for miles. Walter would repeatedly ask his dad to stop waving his arms about in case he scared the fish.

There was the time when Mr Wigmore was trying to enjoy a lovely homemade blackcurrant jam sandwich when a wasp decided it wanted a share. Walter's dad got so angry at the black and yellow striped pest that he took a swipe at it with his sandwich, losing grip and sending the bread and blackcurrant preserve delight, flying into the pond to the grateful applause of clapping mallard duckbills. It was hilarious in hindsight, but at the time, Walter was infuriated with all the fish frightening commotion caused.

The wonderful thing about daydreaming is that it can take you back to a specific time, and for a moment, you are there. Pity then that one can't go back and put things right before they happened, there would be an awful lot of hurt and unnecessary humiliation erased from history!

Hurt and humiliation were no strangers to Walter Wigmore, and the knowledge of that was an upsetting side effect of daydreaming. Even when trying to think of nice events in his life, cruelty would poke its ugly face into most facets of Walter's daydreams. Walter was a good man who bore no malice toward his tormentors, outwardly at least. Gentleness would appear to be a weakness in the bully's eye. Gentleness and humility are good attributes, but to be that very way all the time can make one an easy target.

'Only show your soft side when it's necessary son, don't make it easy for people to see your heart for they will break it!' Walter's father would often say, a father who was painfully aware of his son's meekness. A father who could see much of his younger self in his son, a father who hoped his son would never suffer in the same way as his younger self did.

However, Walter had suffered throughout his life, people that took an immediate dislike to him, people that ridiculed him and so called friends that turned against him in case others thought that they were like him. In the end, none of this mattered much to Walter really, those people were invariably horrible and not the sort he would want to meet on a social basis.

Unbeknown to Walter, both of his sons had to endure ridicule from other children at school because they thought that he was an odd father. That knowledge would have hurt him deeper than any personal ridicule he had ever received, the thought of his beloved boys suffering because of his eccentricity would have torn him apart.

Surfacing from his daydream, Walter became aware of a presence near him. This presence became more evident once the loud bum trumpeting theme tune composed by Graham 'Gruffer' Wheeldon started to play. Did I say composed? Perhaps that should have been decomposed!

"Whoops sorry chum, I couldn't stifle that one!" Gruffer apologized insincerely.

Walter looked back at Gruffer as he stood behind him, trying to find the words to say, to impart his dire disappointment and abhorrence.

"Hey Walter, you've got a bite!" said Gruffer pointing at Walter's now vanished float.

Walter picked up his rod and struck into what seemed to be a bit more than a tiddler. In less than a minute, a 1lb 2oz roach graced the folds of Walter's landing net.

"That's a lovely roach Walter!" said Gruffer excitedly.

"Yes it is indeed Graham, and one of the finest I have ever caught." agreed Walter.

"Chuck some more maggots in, there may be more to catch." Graham advised. Walter did so. The float settled gently, and Walter hunched over his rod with the expectancy of a heron.

"Br-r-r-r-a-pppp!" said Gruffer's posterior.

Walter's float dipped once again, this time he caught a roach of 12oz.

After a few more roach of around the same size, it became apparent that a pattern was forming. Gruffer would break wind, Walter would blench in horror, and then the float would go under to herald the arrival of another end of season roach.

Walter began to wonder if the rumours of Gruffer's flatulent magic were true.

Gruffer had only turned up to have a look at the pond to see how frozen it was, soon after he made his leave by bidding Walter fond adieu with another loud botty song.

Walter caught another wonderful roach of 1lb 6oz, and then all sport dried up.

Once the air had cleared, Walter tried and tried to catch another roach. However, he failed to impress rutilus rutilus with his angling skills and charming maggots.

Walter heard heavy footfalls approaching along the bank side footpath.

"Hello Walter! How are you doing?" said a voice from behind.

It was Rick Western.

"Hello! Is that you Rick?" asked Walter.

"Yeah it is." Rick confirmed.

"Oh, I didn't recognize you, you look different somehow." said Walter.

"Ah ha ha! That'll be the lack of makeup!" laughed Rick.

Rick went on to explain to Walter that he, Jed Clemson and Will Spring only wore makeup to ward people off from fishing the night at Spigworth so that they would get peace and quiet and the pond to themselves.

"But your clothes weren't exactly masculine were they Rick?" questioned Walter.

"The same thing, I don't think army surplus would have been as convincing and it frightened people way." said Rick.

"I wouldn't need to do that, just being myself seems to do the trick." said Walter.

"Some people can be cruel at times Walter, and you don't need them anyway so don't worry about them. As long as you have a core of close friends or family, that is all that matters." said Rick.

Rick was back in Spinfield for a while and thought he would have a look at the old pond again for old time's sake.

"Have you caught anything Walter?" asked Rick.

"Oddly enough I have, I have caught quite a few very nice roach today, I can't claim full merit for my success as I was aided by Graham Wheeldon." said Walter.

"What old Gruffer and his magic bum?" laughed Rick.

"Um, yes." said Walter with slight embarrassment.

"You don't believe all that old guff do you Walter, excuse the pun?" asked Rick.

"Well, every time he broke wind I seemed to get a bite with a good roach on the end of the line." explained Walter.

"Listen Walter, I've had that man sitting next to me, blowing off all afternoon and not caught a thing when I was fishing for roach." said Rick.

"You mean that I may well have caught the fish regardless?" asked Walter.

"Yes, most definitely." said Rick with a confident nod.

Rick looked at Walter's pike rod and noticed that line was slowly being taken from the spool of his reel.

"I'm sorry if I've distracted you, but I think you ought to pick your pike rod up, you've got a take!" Rick alerted Walter.

Walter turned his reel handle to close the bail arm and quickly reeled in until he felt a solid resistance.

The pond erupted as a very angry pike smashed the surface with its tail.

"Oh my goodness, it's huge!" Walter said with a tremble in his voice.

"It most certainly is Walter, you'll have to play this one carefully, I think it's only lightly hooked." said Rick.

Rick looked at Walter's landing net and thought that it may not be adequate to land such a big fish.

"I think you'll need a bigger landing net Walter, I'll get mine from the back of the car." said Rick as he ran up the footpath.

Walter felt very vulnerable and alone as he tussled with the huge pike, convinced that he was going to lose it. It seemed forever waiting for Rick, and Walter had fears that Rick may not return. In reality, Rick had been no longer than three minutes and arrived back at Walter's swim, extremely puffed out and cursing his poor lifestyle of cigarettes and alcohol.

Rick took Walter's landing net off the pole and replaced it with his carp net. Walter played the pike with trepidation and circumspect, the fish had already attempted to shake the hook by tail-walking and vicious shakes of the head, the fight was not over yet.

"I have to say Rick, this is possibly the most frightening tussle I've ever had with a fish." whimpered Walter.

"No need to worry, she looks as though she's tiring quite a bit, she'll be in the net soon." Rick assured Walter.

The pike had other ideas as it made a powerful run and stripped of ten yards of line from Walter's reel.

"She doesn't seem very tired to me Rick." said Walter.

"That'll be the last run; she'll come in like a lamb soon!" Rick said firmly to help calm Walter down.

Just as Rick said, the pike did indeed tire. Very shortly after, Walter was guiding the pike over the landing net that Rick was holding. Just as the pike's tail passed over the front of the net, the hook pulled out catapulting Walter's sprat bait up into the air to land rudely onto his hat. Rick pulled the landing net up to support the weight of a thrashing and angry pike.

"Well at least you won't have to unhook this blighter Walter!" laughed Rick.

"Thank you very much for your help Rick." said Walter with a tear in his eye.

"You're welcome. Now let's weigh the pike." said Rick.

"Um, I've got this spring balance here." said Walter displaying the tiniest of scales Rick had ever seen.

"I think you'll need something a bit more special than that Walter, it only goes up to 15lbs." said Rick.

"I never expect to catch anything that big so I've not found the need to upgrade on certain items of tackle." explained Walter.

"Always expect the unexpected and think big Walter, you just never know what is going to pick your bait up!" said Rick with authority.

"My word, do you think it's that big?" asked an astonished Walter.

"Getting on for twenty I reckon, I'll go and get my scales." said Rick.

Rick took the landing net head off the pole and collapsed the arms so that a couple of wraps of net were securely holding the pike in.

"Here you are Walter, grab hold of the net and lower the pike into the water while I go and get my weighing scales, it won't get out if you keep the net wrapped around the landing net arms." said Rick.

Walter had a few heart racing moments as the pike thrashed about in the net in the shallow margins of Spigworth Pond, but within a few minutes, Rick arrived with a set of dial scales and a camera. It's a pity he hadn't thought about that when he went to get his landing net, the steaming great nit!

Rick weighed the pike for Walter.

"Right, that's 28lbs 15oz, take off the weight of the wet net, which makes her 27lbs exactly." said Rick with a friendly smile.

Rick took a couple of photographs of Walter holding the pike, only the first photo was any good, the second one caught Walter laying on his back with a gill flaring angry pike on his chest as he tried to cradle the fish in his arms.

With the pike returned safely, Walter watched her swim away; it was like seeing the love of one's life leaving for good, never to see her again.

"I very much doubt that I will be able to match today's sport for the rest of this week Rick." said Walter with thoughts of quitting while he was ahead.

"I doubt whether anyone will Walter, I heard the weather forecast for the rest of this week is going to be subzero at night and not much above freezing during the daytime." explained Rick.

That was true; Walter fished the last possible day of that season, the pond remained frozen for the rest of March. Rick asked for Walter's address so that he could drop a photo of his pike in when the film was developed.

At 7:30pm, April 14th 1976, The S.C.A.C conducted an Annual General Meeting at Spigworth Village Hall. Apart from the usual 'Apologies for Absence' and some boring old twerp conducting a lecture on how important it is to maintain the health of the population of swan mussels in your fishery, there was also a dreary presentation of trophies for the match fishing fraternity of the club.

First Prize went to Nobby 'Bleak Snatcher' Whistleton for his gargantuan catch of bleak and a big chub at an away match on the River Wither. 8lbs 3oz and 3 drams was the winning weight, a lot of hard work considering the size of those little fellas, and seemingly impossible for a 4-hour match. Nobby retired from match fishing some time later after his GP diagnosed him with Repetitive Strain Injury due to too much casting out and reeling in bleak. Nobby did try for other species but failed miserably.

Second Prize went to Julie Rathergood for her amazing 18lb 10z catch of Bream on the River Barron during a Christmas charity match for The Spinfield Victim's of Bicycle Theft Society. There was an argument from other women at the AGM that Julie should have received First Prize in a separate women's section. Club secretary Bill Wilton quashed the debate by saying that the prizes were based on catch weight and to have a separate section for women would be sexist. The term 'sexist' wasn't really understood by anyone at the meeting, but there were a lot of 'hear, hear, hears' grunted out from the old farts of the club.

Third prize went to Robin Flick for not falling into Spigworth Pond during a match after a heavy night on the ale. Robin would often turn up to matches still roaring drunk from the night before, often times only casting just before the final whistle, but nearly always getting a soaking as he collapsed face first into the pond during the match. It was no mean feat for Robin to stay dry at a fishing match!

However, after all the pomp and self-preening pretentiousness of trophy presentation, there was a new addition to the prize ceremony. It was very apparent that Spigworth Pond boasted some significant specimen fish in its depths. Therefore, the committee suggested a specimen fish of the year award for the anglers who endure the long blank days and nights in the quest for the 'Big Kipper'! Bill Wilton thought it would be a good idea, because frankly, match fishing bored him brainless!

Bill announced the new award.

"Tonight, it gives me great pleasure to present a new award. The award is called 'The Big Kipper of the Year Award' and goes to the angler who has, by a panel of judges, achieved the most impressive catch of a specimen fish." said Bill.

There were yawns and shouts of 'Get on with it!' from those who wanted to retire to the bar. Bill continued his pre-presentation speech regardless.

"As I say, it is indeed a great pleasure to present this award, and there is no greater pleasure for me than to tell you that the Big Kipper plaque goes to…Walter Wigmore for his fantastic specimen pike of 27lbs from Spigworth Pond." said Bill cheerily.

Walter sat there completely oblivious that someone had called his name out. It didn't help matters that boos, jeers and jealous shouts of 'fluke' and 'jammy git' filled the air, Walter didn't realize the award was for him.

Walter felt a hand on his shoulder as a voice came from behind "Go on Walter, that award is yours!" It was little Peter 'Squirt' Burt.

"Pardon? Hello Peter, what did you say?" asked Walter.

"I said that the award is yours, go up and get it!" Squirt shouted.

Walter timidly walked to the presentation stand, not fully appreciating the significance of his achievement.

The award was magnificent; it was a picture frame with an enlarged photograph of the shot taken by Rick Western of Walter and his pike. Underneath was a little brass plate with an engraved inscription:-

Big Kipper Award 1976
Walter Wigmore and his pike of 22lbs caught from
Spigworth Pond,
a new pond record.

A well deserved prize for your efforts, well done Walter!

This honour completely overwhelmed Walter and he had nothing to say but 'thank you!' For a brief moment in his life, Walter Wigmore felt important and special, a fine end to his coarse fishing season and something to behold for the rest of his life.

The future coarse fishing seasons had mixed success for Walter; he was hailed the pike hero of the S.C.A.C. with an unbroken record for many years, even though he didn't catch another single one! Happily, in October 1992, Walter's son Steven smashed his record with a mammoth pike of 29lbs 13oz. Walter became very ill by then and the S.C.A.C. awarded him an honorary membership for being a nice chap. He fished very little after that, in 1994 Walter sadly passed away in Spinfield General Hospital from complications of heart surgery. Retired club secretary Bill Wilton organized the placement of a memorial bench for Walter behind peg 13, with an inscription:-

In Memory of Walter Wigmore,
a pike hero and a jolly good egg!'

Peter 'Squirt' Burt married Janice Pragnell and begat a lovely family. They named their first born, a lovely little boy, Walter.

Mark Gosling married Christine Blanchette, and lived and fished happily together. Mark even managed to put his miserable git of a bailiff face on at times just to warn off young anglers who misbehaved.

Graham 'Gruffer' Wheeldon carried on breaking wind and reeling in many specimen roach; he continued to be barred from quite a few country alehouses for making a nasty pong during lunchtimes.

Badger Bill Parsons gave up tench fishing to pursue his other love, bird watching, ornithologically speaking of course!

In the 1980s, carp fishing became en vogue when Kenny Maddog and Larry Puddletown gave the angling world their knowledge of the hair rig, Rod Hawkinson was running a very successful carp bait and tackle business and Richwind shelf life boiled baits revolutionized the world of angling nationwide. Everyone became a carp angler for a while, until the carp wised up to everything but the thoughtful rig and bait presentation. This brought back the real angler, the angler with the gift of wisdom, stealth and watercraft.

The S.C.A.C. membership dwindled due to many anglers intrigue in the heavily stocked day ticket waters that opened up seemingly overnight. Spigworth was difficult to fish, but for £6 per day and a bag of shelf life boilies on a day ticket water, mediocre anglers could go home with the pretention that they were a brilliant anglers. Everyone stood a chance of decent sport on the day ticket waters. In addition, when the fishing became difficult, the landowners and unscrupulously lucrative famers would fill their ponds up with even more carp to increase the catch potential, and therefore more revenue.

In 1999, the lease of Spigworth Pond had expired and the landowners Ganderbrath Ltd gave the S.C.A.C. the opportunity to renew it. They chose to relinquish the lease as the landowners were asking too much for a fading club with few members or revenue.

By 2001, the Spigworth Pond lease was up for grabs and a syndicate of ex S.C.A.C. and Binchester Angling Society members stumped up enough money to secure the pond for their greedy selves for 25 years.

Rick Western, Jed Cleminson and Will Spring became part of the syndicate in the vain attempt to recapture the Spigworth spirit of the 1970s, they didn't.

That spirit would never come again!